T0084416

THE POSSIBILITY OF MUSIC

THE POSSIBILITY OF MUSIC

STEPHEN-PAUL MARTIN

TUSCALOOSA

The University of Alabama Press
Tuscaloosa, Alabama 35487-0380

Copyright 2007 by Stephen-Paul Martin
All rights reserved
First Edition

Published by FC2, an imprint of the University of Alabama Press, with support provided by Florida State University and the Publications Unit of the Department of English at Illinois State University

Address all editorial inquiries to: Fiction Collective Two, Florida State University, c/o English Department, Tallahassee, FL 32306-1580

☺

The paper on which this book is printed meets the minimum requirements of American National Standard for Information Sciences—Permanence of Paper for Printed Library Materials, ANSI Z39.48–1984

Library of Congress Cataloging-in-Publication Data
Martin, Stephen-Paul
    The possibility of music / by Stephen-Paul Martin. — 1st ed.
        p. cm.
    ISBN-13: 978-1-57366-134-8 (pbk. : alk. paper)
    ISBN-10: 1-57366-134-1 (pbk. : alk. paper)
    I. Title.
    PS3563.A7292P67 2007
    813'.54—dc22
                                                    2006029455

Cover Design: Lou Robinson
Book Design: Leah Jamison and Tara Reeser
Typeface: Baskerville
Produced and printed in the United States of America

for
the Little Head
and the quadrupeds

ACKNOWLEDGMENTS

Thanks to Hal Jaffe and Mel Freilicher for their perceptive responses to earlier versions of these stories.

The stories in this book have appeared in the following publications: *Arpeggio*, *Fiction International*, *The Journal of Experimental Fiction*, *Muse Apprentice Guild*, *Poetic Inhalations*, *Titanic Operas*, and *Western Humanities Review*.

Collapsing into a Story and *A New Kind of Happiness* originally appeared in the Obscure Publications chapbook series.

OTHER BOOKS BY STEPHEN-PAUL MARTIN

Apparently, Obscure Publications, 2006 (novella)

A New Kind of Happiness, Obscure Publications, 2004 (novella)

Instead of Confusion, Asylum Arts, 2002 (fiction)

Collapsing into a Story, Obscure Publications, 2001 (novella)

Pictures of Nothing, Obscure Publications, 2001 (fiction)

Gaps in the System, Margin to Margin Press, 1999 (fiction)

Not Quite Fiction, Vatic Hum Press, 1997 (fiction)

Undeserved Reputations, Texture Press, 1995 (fiction)

Fear & Philosophy, Detour Press, 1993 (fiction)

The Gothic Twilight, Asylum Arts, 1992 (fiction)

The Flood, The Runaway Spoon Press, 1991 (novella)

Crisis of Representation, Standing Stones Press, 1991 (fiction)

Invading Reagan, Generator Press, 1990 (poetry)

Tales, Paradigm Press, 1990 (fiction)

ADVANCINGreceding, The Runaway Spoon Press, 1989 (poetry)

Things, Heaven Bone Press, 1989 (poetry)

Corona 2500, Score Press, 1989 (poetry)

Until It Changes, The Runaway Spoon Press, 1988 (poetry)

Open Form & the Feminine Imagination, Maisonneuve Press,
     1988 (nonfiction)

Poems, Third Eye Press, 1983 (poetry)

Edges, The New York Literary Press, 1978 (poetry)

CONTENTS

IMPOSSIBLE

Which is most remarkable: making something unreal from unreal materials, making something unreal from real materials, or making something real from unreal materials? This question can best be answered by imagining a science-fiction movie in which beings from a distant planet, or perhaps from another dimension, land on Earth by mistake, in a park in New York City, and quickly find themselves bored by human behavior. They're eager to leave, and plan to do so as soon as they can repair the steering mechanism of their ship.

The earth people panic at first, assuming that the extraterrestrials are dangerous and have come to earth to destroy or subjugate the human race. The armed forces are mobilized and civil defense instructions are broadcast, even though the aliens come out of their ship several times to calmly explain that they're only here by mistake and plan to leave as soon as possible. Human leaders don't even consider the possibility that their visitors might be unimpressed by what they've seen so far.

What do the space people look like? They look roughly like human beings because human beings assume that all advanced life forms have a head, two arms and two legs. The space people carefully explain this misconception, using their superior intelligence to make their language sound like English. But even the greatest human scientists have trouble understanding that beings that look human and seem to be speaking English don't normally look and speak like anything humans can imagine.

The movie's main character, an underpaid lab technician played by an ex-minor-league third-base coach named Frank Acid, frequently watches the extraterrestrials on TV news programs. He's disappointed that he never gets to see the alien spacecraft, and he's baffled by the explanation newscasters provide, that the ship emits a subtle glow that TV cameras can't record. But footage of the ship's crew is shown on a regular basis, allowing him to study the facial expressions and body language the outer space people so convincingly project. After repeated viewings, he thinks he can see past their human façades. He concludes that even though they're being careful to present a polite surface, they're annoyed and bored with the anxious attention they've been receiving. In fact, they may have been disgusted by the human race long before they were forced to land on the earth, having studied the species from their own distant planet.

He writes a long letter published in *The New York Times* explaining his theory, but letters of response from readers all over the nation harshly attack his ideas, claiming that beings millions of light-years from home would surely be amazed at a world so different from their own, even if they had already seen Earth from a distance. He gets an even more dismissive reaction from colleagues at the chemistry lab and especially from his personal friends, who laugh in his face and tell him that he's projecting onto the aliens his own contempt for the human race. One friend even gives him the name of a therapist.

Their laughter triggers painful memories involving family members, former teachers, and ex-girlfriends, scenes that speed up and slow down and run in reverse, accompanied by jarring free-form jazz, alternate versions of the same composition playing at the same time, keeping him awake three nights in a row. At one a.m. on the third night, he staggers out of bed and goes for a walk. The camera carefully follows him through the city, focusing on his reflections in moonlit shop fronts, the shadows of his body and the shadows of the buildings on the pavement, turning what would be a mere interlude in most films into an adventure in visual motion, suggesting perhaps that he likes to wander, or that he's trapped in a mental maze he can't or doesn't want to solve. The audience would normally expect soundtrack music at this point, since there's no dialogue, no interpersonal conflict. But the film's director, a self-proclaimed eccentric, likes to spring aesthetic surprises, so as the lab technician walks, there's nothing but the sound of his shoes on the sidewalk, echoing off the walls of towering buildings. The sound becomes hypnotic, and the scene takes almost fifteen minutes, as if to challenge the assumption that transitions are less important than what they connect.

At length he comes to the park where the aliens landed, and viewers are free to assume that the lab technician hasn't really been wandering, that he knew from the start that he wanted to see the ship. Of course, it's carefully guarded, surrounded by tanks, lights, and barbed wire fences. But he knows the park well enough to sneak around the guards and hide himself behind a large rock on a wooded hill, which gives him an unobstructed view of the ship. He sits nervously at first, and it's clear from a quick sequence of flashback scenes that he's uneasy about the bulletins issued by government and military officials, warning thrill-seekers and tabloid reporters to stay away. This might be a perfect time to build suspense with ominous music. But again the director avoids the obvious, and there's nothing but the sound of steady breeze in late spring leaves.

Slowly the lab technician begins to relax, mesmerized by the changing shape of the ship, which looks like an oval mirror, then like a wineglass, a corncob pipe, a kettledrum, a megaphone, a pyramid, a waterfall. The transformations never stop, and viewers are left to wonder why: Is it because the space people want to conceal their ship's true shape, or because the notion of a true shape is alien to the people who built the ship, or because the ship was built in a timeless world, and now that it's trapped in a place controlled by temporal changes, it can only avoid slipping into the past by changing into something else, or because it's collecting information from all over the world, taking the shapes of the objects it's observing, scanning the globe with recording technologies that exceed anything humans can even imagine? There's no way to be sure. But the shapes often change without completing themselves, without remaining stable enough to convey a firm visual message, as if their primary function were to make description obsolete.

At this point whispered narration begins, initially indistinguishable from the breeze, but slowly taking the form of the lab technician's thoughts about the ship. He begins to suspect that it's not just a vehicle of transportation, but also a form of expression, a language made of one evolving signal. He's intrigued that the aliens may have come from a place where traveling and language are the same thing. But he's haunted by the suspicion that his attention is too intrusive, that it's changing what he's looking at, that he's changing himself by changing what he's looking at. Nonetheless he keeps looking, as if he were under a spell, as if the ship were compelling him to cast a spell on himself.

Although he's never tried to translate anything, he thinks he's beginning to see what some of the changing shapes might mean, even if they can't be summarized in simple human terms. It finally occurs to him that the extraterrestrials might have no separate existence, that they might be nothing outside of their ship, nothing outside of their language, that they function like words and ideas, that they're not confined by space and time. But then he dozes off on the rock, sleeping into the sunrise. When he wakes up, he looks perplexed, angry with himself, and captions flashed across the bottom of the screen tell the audience that he remembers only the general outlines of his thinking, and none of the specific insights he got from his night of translation. He's beside himself: How could he forget something so important, something which might have changed the fate of the earth? All the mistakes he's ever made become a composite image, a huge mosquito biting through his forehead, sucking out his brain. But as he hurries home to get ready for work, he remains convinced that major understandings might be developed if professional translators, or perhaps cryptographers, were hired to study the ship's evolving shape.

At this point, normal cinematic logic would call for a quick transition. But once again, the director stands the film on its head, focusing for ten minutes on the lab technician rushing home, bumping into people and apologizing, getting yelled at by people who won't accept the apologies, losing his way, going down the same wrong street three times, barely escaping a raging German shepherd, getting temporarily blinded by the glare of sunlight on the chrome of a passing school bus. When he finally gets home, he picks up the phone and battles his way through bureaucratic obstacles and evasions until he's talking with a well-known astrophysicist, urging him to study the ship in linguistic terms, like an archaeologist having unearthed a text in a language no living person has ever seen before. The scientist tries to be nice, listens patiently, but ends up laughing, telling the lab technician that he needs a good night's sleep.

This condescending dismissal drives him to sit on the edge of his bed and stare at the floor. The rookie actor Frank Acid does a wonderful job, indicating in silence, through facial expressions alone, that the moment is bringing back memories of the lab technician's father, or rather his grandfather, or rather his great-grandfather, or rather his great-great-grandfather, about whom he knows nothing. This means that the memory is a blank space, an emptiness so unnerving that it can only be compared to people visiting a zoo of numbers, integers and fractions pacing back and forth in their cages, parents making patient explanations for their children, convinced that displays of captivity can be educational, while other people sit on benches, wiping their brows, not sure how to count anymore, not sure what it means to make mistakes in long division, eating hot dogs covered with relish and mustard, killing mosquitoes feasting on their foreheads, paging through colorful guidebooks that slowly burn their fingers, while the sound of a bellowing monster approaches from a distance, a sound that everyone quickly connects with music, a barge of jazz musicians on a slow polluted river, a sound that backdrops one of the movie's most poignant moments, as the lab technician tries to convince an unsympathetic friend on the phone that they live in a world where no one understands anything.

He hangs up and stares at the bare floor, watching a large cockroach dash out from under a battered couch, stopping to feast on a pellet of spilled rice. He makes no move to crush it, shows no disturbance at all. The cockroach runs back under the couch, comes out again briefly, runs in a figure eight, or perhaps an infinity sign, then dashes under the bathroom door. The lab technician's face remains impassive. The whispered narration begins again, as if in response to the roach, though the words have nothing to do with insects, and everything to do with the lab technician's idea that the outer space people aren't limited by time and space, at least not in ways that humans can recognize. If this is true, then why do they need to repair their steering device? Why do they need a steering device at all? Can't the mere thought of home become their home? Isn't their ship of language a universe in itself? He decides that the broken steering device is nothing more than an unforeseen gap or defect in their language, though he knows that he's using human terms and human syntax to think about something that probably can't be described in human language. In other words, he's completely lost, and the whispered narration begins to sound like radio static, interference coming from his personal past, from insecurities and disturbing memories that often emerge when he's baffled.

It's at this moment that the film most fully separates itself from other sci-fi movies of the period. Where many sci-fi directors work with characters forced to face the scorn of scientific authorities, the director of this film devotes large portions of the narrative to the main character's battle with his own doubts and limitations. The lab technician is unclear about his role in the world, suffering from a sense of alienation that often feels overwhelming but also inauthentic, as if it were simply another part to play. To make matters worse, the skeptical perceptions that lead him to question the authenticity of his alienation also appear to be scripted, and seem to have emerged from a system of belief, a firm conviction that critical evaluation is an absolute necessity in every aspect of existence, which is of course problematic, since belief systems and absolute necessities imply a bedrock of certainty that goes against the need to question everything.

How does Frank Acid convey this convoluted state of mind? With grave difficulty. He feels like his life is taking place in a rearview mirror. After all, he's trapped in the task of acting like someone who consistently functions at a distance from himself, a role that would baffle even the most experienced actor, let alone someone who's not an actor by trade. In fact, he got the lead role in this film only because the director is an old friend and owes him a favor. Why didn't the director, eager to build his reputation, hire someone famous and find another way to pay Frank Acid back? Because he knew Frank Acid badly needed money, and besides, his well-publicized approach is to find people who aren't actors to play the main characters in his films, putting Hollywood superstars in supporting roles. This strategy has been quite effective in the past, forcing viewers to watch the film itself, unable to focus on celebrities in the customary way. It also appeals to the stars, who get paid their normal fee without having to do much of anything. But Frank Acid finds the experience painful. At times he thinks he's losing his mind, collapsing under the pressure of pretending to be an actor, feeling weird about inhabiting a fictive identity, surrounded by people who aren't pretending to be in the acting business, people who like nothing more than acting like someone who doesn't exist.

Things get so bad that about halfway through the process of shooting the film, after a frustrating afternoon of doing the same scene fifteen times and still not getting it right, it occurs to Frank Acid that human perception is based on a fundamental misunderstanding. Where people have always assumed that they lived in four dimensions, he suddenly sees that reality takes place in six dimensions. In addition to three spatial dimensions, we also inhabit three dimensions of time: past, present, and future. This insight seems so obvious that he can't see why anyone ever believed in only four dimensions. Of course, even the concept of four dimensions was controversial at first, when Einstein first proposed it. But now the notion is so widely accepted that it blocks people from seeing the truth. At first Frank Acid resists his own insight, telling himself that past and future lack the solid qualities of the three spatial dimensions, and that time exists as a single entity, a process of duration. But he knows this makes no sense, that it overlooks the very powerful realities imposed on us by memory and anticipation, by history and prediction. It also overlooks the extent to which the present tense is really just a paper-thin transition between what's already happened and what hasn't happened yet.

So why do we cheat ourselves by pretending to live in only one temporal dimension? How long will we continue to favor space over time? How can we learn to avoid the mistakes of the past and generate a more enlightened future if we keep acting as if time is one-dimensional? Once Frank Acid sees the truth, he's angry that he's been trained to see the world in such a self-defeating way. But he's also unnerved by the prospect of learning how to perceive all over again. He'd rather just go back to the four-dimensional world that everyone else inhabits. He's already got his own problems to confront. He doesn't need more complexity. But he can't deny the truth, and he can't pretend that it won't involve complex psychological changes. Suddenly the film seems pointless. It's only out of loyalty to his friend that he keeps himself from walking away. But he firmly concludes that he never wants to appear on screen again, turning his back on a career that could have made him rich and famous.

Once the film is in the can, he decides not to see the completed version. He avoids the final screening. But one night his wife tells him that he's a worthless piece of shit, that she's tired of his talk about six dimensions, tired of being married to a guy who always finds excuses to run away from his opportunities, that he could have been a great minor-league third-base coach if he'd only been willing to stand up for himself in confrontations with his colleagues, that he could have been more than a minor-league third-base coach if he'd only been willing to pursue his education, that he could soon become a mass media superstar if he would only take small steps to develop his acting career. Her tirade lasts all day, and he needs a break. He's badly shaken. He needs firm proof that he's not a complete loser, and he can think of only one way to restore his confidence: by returning to the scene of his disturbing revelation, facing himself by watching himself on-screen.

As he approaches the movie house on Houston Street in lower Manhattan, it occurs to Frank Acid that he'd better disguise himself if he wants to watch the film without being recognized. Though he's not a famous actor, the film has been getting rave reviews. He's seen huge pictures of himself on billboards all over the city, in full-page ads in magazines and the daily papers. His public face offends him, since it bears little resemblance to what he sees in the bathroom mirror, and he doesn't know why anyone would make the connection between the two faces. Nonetheless, he wants to be sure he can watch himself on screen in peace, without being bothered by autograph seekers. So he buys a baseball hat and wrap-around shades in the nearby variety store, then stands in a long line to buy his ticket.

It's cold and rainy, and the baseball hat doesn't offer much protection. But the rain is the least of his problems. The fact that he's trying not to be recognized fills him with an eerie feeling, reminding him of his childhood in Brooklyn, when he would have done anything to be recognized for the A's he got in high school physics. But his father, whose main claim to fame was that his grandfather died with Custer at the Little Bighorn River, kept his eyes on his two older brothers because they were all-star baseball players. Frank Acid tried to pretend that he too was obsessed with baseball, even after his lack of talent was obvious, even after his father died, even after his wife pointed out that he was trying to please a phantom, that he might as well do what he really cared about, learn to be the man he thought he really was, or might be. He told her that she sounded like a pop psychology book. She told him that his life was like a pop psychology book. He told her that he was too smart for therapeutic formulas, a stance he maintains to this day. But it doesn't change the feeling that's been with him all his life, that he was born on the wrong planet, that he's like a number trapped in a cage, that his life would make more sense in another dimension. The rain drips off the visor of his hat and lands at the base of his neck, reminding him that he's still in disguise, waiting in line to watch himself pretend to be someone else.

When the movie starts he's struck by the difference between the fragmented feeling he developed during the shooting, acting in a series of individual scenes with only a vague sense of the plot as a whole, and the well-paced narrative motion that the editors have produced. He can't connect himself with the impression he makes on screen, the way his words combine with the soundtrack to seem more impressive than he remembers them being in the script, and certainly more impressive than he sounds in everyday life. He thinks that if he could sound cinematically forceful when he talks to his wife, she might accept his lack of ambition, his feeling that nothing is worth doing, that the human race is a joke that goes flat long before the person telling it stops laughing, or a joke that fails because of bad narrative timing, or a joke that's a lot meaner than the situation calls for, or a joke that everyone's already heard and wasn't that good in the first place.

But aside from the amplified sound of his voice, Frank Acid isn't impressed by the character he's playing, or by any of the other humans in the film. He strongly favors the extraterrestrials, their annoyance in confronting human arrogance, their growing desire to leave Earth as quickly as possible. He feels this same desire so intensely that he finally gets up and leaves, missing the final third of the movie, walking without an umbrella through a night of freezing rain. At times the whispered narratives from the film replace the voice that talks to him in his head, and when he returns to his own thoughts, he sounds like someone else, like he landed by mistake in the mind of someone he doesn't like. After three hours of wandering, he decides to take his own life by jumping off the Brooklyn Bridge.

Meanwhile, back in the movie house, everyone is anxious, waiting for the space people to become aggressive and monstrous, justifying the fears of the human race. But nothing happens. The extraterrestrials remain aloof, wanting only to repair their ship in peace. Their ship remains a changing shape that cameras can't quite capture. As the movie reaches its final phase, the big problem for the scientific and military communities, and indeed for the entire population of the planet, is to face a fact that's becoming increasingly clear, that the space people have no interest in the human race and feel annoyed by human attempts to communicate with or study them. The lab technician is convinced that the only sane way to handle this horrible feeling is to confront it with rigorous honesty and try to learn from it. But he knows that no one in a position of power is strong enough to take this approach, and he's not willing to make a case for it himself, not after having been laughed at so viciously a month before.

In his most recent night in the park, the lab technician deduced from the ship's evolving shape that the aliens' problem was nearly solved, that they had found the hidden defects in their syntax, that all their confused revisions were finally falling into place. But now he can't bring himself to publish this new concept in a letter to the *Times*, reading all the contemptuous responses, confronting his personal pain all over again, having his best friends tell him that he needs to see a shrink. Before the ship landed, he generally kept his ideas to himself, not wanting to cast his pearls before swine. It was only the urgency of the situation that drove him to publish his thoughts a few weeks before. Now he's got a perfect excuse to withdraw from the rest of the world. But when he has lunch with his mother, an unemployed math professor, in a café near his apartment building, she tells him that people need to hear what he has to say, and that he'll get a more enlightened response if he sends his theories to *Scientific American*, even if he doesn't initially reach as many readers.

The screen is silent as the camera shoots him sitting at his desk, typing the same letter over and over again, crumpling and tossing defective pages over his shoulder onto the floor, growling at the keyboard. The camera zooms in several times to show that his prose is quite powerful, gracefully and precisely guiding his thinking down from his mind to the page. But he keeps revising anyway, tearing beautiful sentences apart, a clear indication that his problems have nothing to do with writing, and everything to do with fear of rejection, fear of the kind of laughter that's only one letter away from slaughter. But once he gives up on publishing his theory, he's left with nothing to do but absorb the misguided nonsense of people with credentials. The frustration of watching politicians and astronomers coming up with official evasions and explanations drives him to the brink of suicide.

His rejection of this option is one of the most powerful moments in the movie. It takes place in the lab technician's tiny apartment. He sits on the edge of his bed beside the window, watching roaches making infinity signs on his bare wood floor, then gazing at a poster on his wall: King Kong smashing biplanes from the top of the Empire State Building. The final section of John Coltrane's *A Love Supreme* plays in the background, quietly at first but slowly increasing in volume, a soundtrack technique that's been used in many movies, but now adds so much tension to the moment that time crashes like a battered biplane, like a tower made of syllables hit by lightning. He looks back down at the floor, then at the panel of light and shade on the wall, the way it moves in the breeze coming in through dusty venetian blinds, as if it were a language he could read, as if the whispered monologue that accompanies Coltrane's tenor sax were speaking from the light and shade and also from behind his eyes, telling him that he's trapped in what he's telling himself about himself, that human language is a cage of mirrors, not a house with rooms and doors and windows, and certainly not a way of traveling light-years in a second. The disturbing emptiness of this realization collapses beautifully into the tormented crescendo of Coltrane's music, and also into the not-quite-perfect cheekbones of the lab technician staring out the window at sunlight flashing on the chrome of a passing school bus. He turns away, picks up the phone, and calls the suicide hotline.

The director was apparently aware that Coltrane himself was at the point of suicide, and rejected it only because he felt the grace of a love supreme, a divine force transforming him in ways that few listeners will ever have a chance to musically contemplate, since great composers like Coltrane are carefully excluded from mainstream radio, but this is not the story of a nation driving its most enlightened people mad, nor is it the story of computer sabotage aimed at the media conglomerates of right-wing Christians, focusing closely on a network of hackers who mess up Clear Channel's computers, substituting avant-garde jazz for commercial trash on all the nation's radios at once, an intervention described as terrorist activity on the six o'clock news, nor is it the story of an assassin losing his nerve, letting a dangerous ultra-conservative President survive, letting him keep using taxpayers' money to violently expand his own business empire, and the would-be assassin decides to kill himself because he chickened out, but chickens out again when he tries to shoot and later hang himself, finally getting himself to see a therapist, improving, doing yoga three times a week, falling in love with himself and the world, getting up his nerve again and blowing the President's brains out, nor is it the story of a sentence written only to reach a point where its meaning slips on a banana peel without making anyone laugh, nor is it the story of someone who thinks he's too cool for mass culture, sustaining his ego by telling himself that only morons can tolerate prime-time TV shows and Hollywood movies, only to fall in love with a sitcom actress, who convinces him that he's handsome enough to appear on-screen himself, and soon he's in a coffee commercial featuring progressive jazz, a hip young man in a penthouse apartment reading on a leather couch, steam twisting out of his coffee cup on the low glass table beside him. The use of serious music in degraded commercial contexts is of course one of the most infuriating aspects of contemporary life, and many musicians over the past fifty years have deliberately made their music so difficult and disturbing that advertisers would never think of using it to attract consumers. The final movement of *A Love Supreme* is in this category. It's too urgent, too full of sincere feeling for a commercial. It's tempting to think that the lab technician actually hears the soundtrack music, and that its meaning is clear to him, even though he knows nothing of Coltrane's transformation. And it's tempting to think that if Frank Acid had stayed for the end of the movie, allowing himself to be moved by *A Love Supreme*, he might still be alive today.

The movie ends with the extraterrestrials leaving in disgust, vowing never to go anywhere near Earth again, leaving a message in the sky that everyone finds insulting. The leaders of the world want war, but since they don't where the aliens live and have no weapons that could even reach the moon, no battle plans are developed. Instead, celebrations begin worldwide, people waving flags and singing songs, proclaiming the glories of the human race, as if monsters had been driven off in an epic battle, as if Earth were the only safe and moral place in the universe.

But the message left in the sky descends on the earth, changing from words into rain that seeps into people's bodies and minds. They slowly begin to see the truth, and within a month the entire planet is depressed, deeply disturbed at having been judged so boring and repulsive. Some viewers complain that this ending is too cynical, clearly showing that the director thinks he's too good for the rest of the world. But a hopeful interpretation can also be entertained, based on the assumption that the planet's so-called dominant species has finally been humbled, profoundly humbled, that its depression is really a positive indication, a sign that the human race is prepared to confront its inherent limitations: to see that if two people cannot occupy the same space, and if space cannot be separated from time, then two people cannot occupy the same instant of time, which separates them so fundamentally that they never quite share the same experience, meaning that communication is impossible, though the illusion of communication remains an absolute necessity.

THE POSSIBILITY OF MUSIC

I didn't expect to become a composer. If anything, when I moved to San Diego from New York three years ago, I expected my interest in music to diminish. After all, I was leaving the jazz capital of the world for a place addicted to recreation: swimming, boating, water skiing, scuba diving, hiking, cycling, and especially surfing. True, San Diego had a great jazz radio station, but its transmission signal was so weak that even within the city itself it was hard to get good reception. Driving from one neighborhood to another, I often became enraged when a great saxophone solo got slaughtered by static, or by the intrusion of a top-forty station with a more powerful signal.

Two years later, when the station bought a stronger signal, this kind of interference became less frequent. But the station began compromising itself, selling advertising space to pay for its new transmission power. It never sold out completely. It still played great jazz. The ads it accepted were more dignified, less obnoxious, than what you would hear on a top-forty station. But I could feel the mainstream closing in.

I didn't blame San Diego. The same thing was happening everywhere. Even in New York, a full decade before, the only jazz station in the city had turned into a top-forty station overnight, despite a bitter protest campaign that lasted months. At the time I told myself that I was glad I wasn't a composer, that I wasn't becoming obsolete in a country dominated by stupid music. Over the next ten years things kept getting worse, turning intelligent behavior—aesthetic or otherwise—into an even more marginal phenomenon than it already was. By the time I came to the West Coast in the year 2000, I was amazed that a station financially supported by jazz lovers still existed, especially in a military town like San Diego.

But this was just one weak signal in a blizzard of noise. Everywhere I turned, I saw the triumph of Radio George Bush, otherwise known as Clear Channel. I remember listening to one of my favorite jazz compositions in my apartment, then hearing a Muzak version of it five minutes later in the supermarket. Of course I'd been hating Muzak for a long time. But the sudden juxtaposition of great art with commercial bullshit sent me over the edge. I went to the store's owner and told him exactly how I felt. He sympathized with my rage, telling me that he hated Muzak too. But higher-ups he'd never met had made the decision to play Clear Channel stations in all their stores, and there was nothing he could do about it. No doubt if I'd gone to these higher-ups, they would have said the same thing.

Everyone feels rage when they can't directly confront the people responsible for fucking up their lives. For the most part, this frustration is repressed, expressing itself indirectly, symbolically. But at some point internal pressures explode, and symbolic truth becomes literal truth. Ten years ago, on the Upper West Side of Manhattan, I was listening to John Coltrane's *A Love Supreme*, when I looked out my tenth-floor window at the Twin Towers in the distance. I'd always loved this view, even though the Towers themselves were an obvious symbol of American commerce and its economic domination of the world. Lightning darted from a low cloud, and for maybe five seconds I thought the Towers had been assaulted by the heavens, that the gods had again grown weary of human arrogance. I imagined both Towers burning, then collapsing, while the music made my small apartment seem as large as the city outside. It occurred to me that Trane's long saxophone solo, flashing over the furious drumming of Elvin Jones, was an apocalyptic signal heralding the collapse of media capitalism, ushering in a more compassionate, more intelligent society.

When the Twin Towers actually burned and collapsed a few years ago, I was deeply disturbed. I knew it would not mean the collapse of media capitalism. I knew it would not mean a more compassionate, more intelligent society. I knew the rich would still own the means of image production and the poor would still be stuffed with offensive ads and stupid music. I knew that lots of innocent Americans had been killed and that many innocent non-Americans would soon be killed in retribution. I knew that an already violent, paranoid nation would become even more violent and paranoid. And I knew that jazz would remain a marginal phenomenon.

It may seem absurd to think about jazz in connection with 9/11. After all, the terrorist attacks were a tragic moment in American history, while the ongoing assault on art and intelligence by the mainstream media is so much a part of everyday life in this country that most people don't even notice it. I myself was guilty of this ignorance at times. Since I could generally find the music I wanted in stores or through the Internet, and since no one stopped me from listening to it, for the most part I was content to enjoy what I enjoyed and let others enjoy what they enjoyed. But whenever I thought about the political implications of media capitalism, the way music was used to manufacture a nation of obedient consumers, I got angry. I couldn't sit still. I would have to get out and walk. I almost always ended up at the Pequod, a seaside café I liked because it was a media-free zone—no TVs or Clear Channel stations polluting the atmosphere—and because people I knew regularly met there and talked about music.

On September 12, 2001, I was feeling especially grim about the future of serious music, or of any intelligent form of human expression, for that matter. I felt guilty about living my life as if nothing horrendous had happened the day before, but because of that guilt I felt the need to get out and live my life as if nothing horrendous had happened. The Pequod was the perfect escape. Many of the people I typically met there were jazz musicians and avant-garde composers. I knew they would be too absorbed with their aesthetic concerns to care about Osama bin Ladin.

The last sentence may sound contemptuous. If so, this is not my intention. Or not my sole intention. Yes, we were turning our backs on a national disaster. But in truth there was nothing we could do to make the situation better. And at least the subjects we focused on were harmless, and would no doubt lead some of us to clarify our thinking about confusing artistic issues. Since I wasn't a composer at the time, I didn't go to the café to promote my own ideas. But I loved the atmosphere, the fiercely serious conversations, and I generally left the café with something to think about.

As I walked onto the covered patio that day, noting with pleasure the vast view of the ocean it commanded, I saw that the usual group had already launched into a heated discussion of an issue that had come up many times in the year I'd been going there: What is music, and what should composers be offering their listeners? These seemed like important concerns for individual musicians to contend with, but the assumption that there were general answers to these questions baffled me.

I'd always told myself that if I ever wrote my own music, every composition would become its own distinct struggle with aesthetic questions that emerged as the process unfolded, yielding answers that might or might not be consistent with what I'd come up with in the past. Since I would never know in advance how my own scores would turn out, I didn't see how anyone else could tell me what my goals and aesthetic procedures should be. But I wasn't making my own music at the time, so I never openly objected when my friends at the Pequod talked as if they knew exactly what all authentic composers ought to be doing. Besides, they were fun to listen to, and there was something inspiring about the urgency of their discussions.

Peter, a tall slender man who always looked like he was about to sneeze, insisted that any music that sounded like music wasn't really music, but an imitation of the past. We can't escape the past, he contended, if we condition listeners to expect sound to be organized in traditional ways. Sheldon, a tall slender man who always looked like he was about to fart, got all worked up about Peter's uncritical use of the word *sound*, since music, Sheldon insisted, need not include sound. In fact, his favorite modern composers had defined music as any interval of structured activity, which might or might not involve the use of sound. When Maureen, a tall slender woman who always looked like she was about to cry, objected that Sheldon was being too inclusive, that too many things that had no aesthetic value, like a baseball game or a presidential debate, would qualify as music under Sheldon's definition, Elizabeth, a tall slender woman who always looked like she was about to laugh, cheerfully interrupted with the claim that if a baseball game could be seen as a piece of music, it would be much more interesting, and if fans attended games with aesthetic instead of athletic expectations, it would force the coaches and players to redefine their strategies and performances, a crucial first step toward changing the very nature of competitive activity.

Though I'd heard these arguments before, I always enjoyed the various ways that my companions presented themselves, the weird things they did with their hands when they talked, placing emphasis on selected words and phrases, manipulating their facial expressions. But on September 12, 2001, I could only follow what they were saying with extreme effort, and I thought my time would be better spent if I took a long walk by the sea. The sun was going down, and the colors splashed over the clouds by the fading light had never been more magnificent. But the darkness that followed seemed impatient, unwilling to respect the colors and forms it was dissolving, and the night was filled with the half-seen shapes and motions of a cryptic language meant to be read by no one.

I followed a path up the side of a cliff and paused, amazed by stars that seemed much closer than usual, filling the waves with points of throbbing light. I thought about the well-known celestial paradox, that some of the stars I was looking at weren't there anymore, that their light might have been reaching me from a time before the planet even existed. Then I saw, maybe two hundred yards off-shore, the graceful neck and reptilian head of what could only be the Loch Ness monster. The starlight gave its towering shape such clarity that I knew I wasn't making an incorrect identification. I'd seen photographs and even a short film of the Loch Ness monster, and I knew beyond question what I was looking at—a dinosaur that somehow never died.

Of course I was afraid. But if the monster saw me, it was unconcerned, and after five minutes of scanning the cliffs and oceanfront houses, it slipped back into the sea. I stood on the cliff in shock for almost an hour, afraid that if I moved I would fall and kill myself on the rocks below. I kept scanning the waves for the monster, but saw nothing but reflected starlight rising and falling. Only later did it occur to me that I hadn't been in any serious danger, remembering that dinosaurs of the Loch Ness monster-type were vegetarians.

I hope I don't have to explain that I'm not a tabloid person. I've never been visited by unidentified flying objects, I've never seen Bigfoot or the Abominable Snowman, and I've never had an out-of-body experience. Nor can I explain what a Scottish dinosaur was doing off the California coast. I'd always assumed that "Nessie" was a freshwater creature. It occurred to me, of course, that there was some connection between the terrorist attacks and the monster. And indeed if these events had happened in a work of fiction, readers might be expected to see a symbolic relationship between the two. But there was nothing literary about either occurrence. My first impulse was to notify the authorities. After all, in fifties monster movies, the main character always tells the police or the army about the monster as soon as he can. But invariably, everyone thinks he's crazy, and since I didn't want to face the skeptical faces, I decided not to make a police report.

Instead I went home and searched the Internet for pictures of dinosaurs, and for the latest theories explaining their extinction. I wish I could say that this investigation led me to become so concerned with human extinction that I became an environmental activist, a dedicated member of an organization that blew up factories if they refused to comply with pollution regulations. Or I wish I could say that I woke up the next morning and began a speculative essay about gaps in the fabric of space-time, black holes that allowed ancient creatures to move accidentally from the distant past to the present and even the future, the implication being that time, like space, exists in three dimensions, that the past and future are just as tangibly real as the present, though of course they're not as present, just as width and length are not as tall as height. But I wasn't interested in joining an organized group or putting words on paper. I'd done both many times in the past, back in New York City, and had always come away feeling stupid, like I'd made a fool of myself, though most people were polite enough to pretend they hadn't noticed. Still, as I kept clicking the mouse and staring at the glowing screen, it occurred to me that I could become an activist or a writer without ever dealing with anyone face-to-face. There were so many web sites, so many links between sites, a network of Babel that might someday be destroyed for daring to simulate the complexity of the human mind and the vastness of the universe, reminding me of something a friend once told me, that the number of possible neural connections in the brain exceeds the number of stars in the universe, a concept I still find entertaining, even if it sounds impossible.

But as I kept pointing and clicking, flashing from site to site, I was slowly overtaken by a familiar online feeling, a blurred and slightly exhausted sense of not knowing where I was or what I was looking for. The Net began to seem shallow and dull, especially when I came to a site that claimed to be about extinction but focused instead on the Devil, who apparently was not to be regarded as the source of all evil, nor even as a tragic hero, but as a delusional being struggling through a protracted identity crisis, losing track of himself in a labyrinth of increasingly blurred possibilities, finally redefining himself as a character called God, whose deep insecurities soon drove him to create a place he called the world, and everything went quite well until the creator became unstable again, losing himself once more in a labyrinth of increasingly blurred possibilities, redefining himself as an ape that walked erect and spoke, blurring the meanings of words like *devil* and *god* and *world* and *human*. My sleep that night was a blur of language, which didn't mean that my dreams were filled with people who couldn't stop talking. In fact, I didn't dream at all. In the space where dreamlike images might have surfaced, words were eating and spitting out other words, an activity that was possible because the words had been stripped of their meanings, like a person having his insides emptied out and replaced by heated stones, the final preparation for a trip to another dimension.

The next day my friend Bob and I went to the movies. Bob wasn't part of the Pequod crowd. He avoided them because he thought they were all pretentious jerks. Certainly Bob had strong ideas of his own, but he also had good conversational skills and didn't make people feel stupid if he didn't agree with them. He didn't like jazz, but we shared an interest in avant-garde science fiction, so we went to see a new film deliberately made in black and white, a simulation of a fifties outer space movie, but with a major twist. In your typical fifties UFO movie, the aliens arrive on purpose and plan to conquer the human race, or in the case of *The Day the Earth Stood Still*, to terrorize the U.S.A. and Russia into giving up the atomic bomb. But in this new film, *Impossible*, the aliens have crashed on earth by mistake, and want only to get away from the human race as quickly as possible.

Bob thought it was funny. I thought the humor was too cynical. I could see why beings advanced enough to reach Earth from a distant planet would be disgusted by people. But I didn't like the director's obvious lack of compassion for human stupidity, his dismissive attitude, his refusal to see himself as just another person, driven by the same arrogance that has led our species to the brink of extinction. It seemed to me that the director thought he was too good for the human race, and I found it interesting when Bob later told me that Frank Acid, the novice actor who played the movie's main character, committed suicide soon after the film was made.

The day was cold and rainy, rare for San Diego, but perfect for triggering idealized memories of New York City, so I went home and played *A Love Supreme*, curling up under a blanket next to an open window. I love the feeling of just barely not being cold, just barely being sheltered from severe weather conditions. Cold rain gusted in through the window, tossing the blue silk drapes, making me feel slightly chilly. I followed each Coltrane riff, the sheets of sound that made him famous, a technique that took him two decades to perfect, each phrase becoming a snake eating its tail, splitting into several different versions of itself, like something that looks like a mountain in the sunrise, but looks more like a valley when the shades of evening fall, or something that looks like a city street from a distance, but looks more like a hot dog when it's only three feet away, or something that sounds like a logical treatise when it's being discussed in a classroom, but sounds more like a sermon on predestination when students try to read it on their own, or something that feels like warm breeze when it floats across a flagstone patio, but feels more like a toothache when it shapes a dune a hundred miles from anything like an oasis, and as long as the music played nothing else mattered. Each moment formed itself in place of a billion alternate possibilities, but the music kept them from dissolving, holding them in suspension, like pictures in a darkroom tray that haven't yet been developed, as if the multiplication of images that occurs in facing mirrors were taking place without mirrors, without images. Saxophone melodies dipped and fluttered up and veered like butterflies, while the drumming sounded like a madman trapped in my speakers, trying desperately to break out. It occurred to me that melodies exist only because the mind momentarily rises above the turbulence of the body, the biochemical transformations that somehow become consciousness and language, and Coltrane's horn was conquering temporal sequence only because it was wild and graceful enough to survive the savagery of Elvin Jones's drum kit.

But I was sure if I shared my thoughts with my friends in the café, they would shoot them down right away, first because Coltrane wasn't avant-garde enough anymore, and second because my ideas didn't reveal a full awareness of musical technique and terminology. No doubt their aesthetic sophistication exceeded mine. But I often wondered about their manners, why they felt so free to hurt my feelings, trashing ideas I cared about. To a certain extent, I kept quiet in the café because I didn't want to feel stupid and I knew my friends didn't care if I did. There was more than a little resentment in my silence. But I always felt better when I stopped clinging to my own thinking so tightly, letting myself enjoy the rhetorical strategies, facial expressions and bizarre gestures that came with fierce confrontations between people who never seemed to doubt themselves.

Coltrane himself was filled with doubts, torment that led him to become addicted to smack in the mid-fifties. But in 1957 he had what he called a spiritual awakening, which gave him the strength to kick his habit. I'm skeptical about spiritual awakenings, and the music I expect from people following an encounter with God is the half-assed folk rock that musicians of the Woodstock generation began to make after they became Jesus freaks in the early seventies. But the music of Coltrane's last ten years became increasingly unconventional, as if his divine experience had expanded his powers of aesthetic expression. He began to read books on sub-atomic physics, connecting the insights of quantum mechanics to his compositional practice. Whatever Coltrane meant by a spiritual awakening, it didn't include the banal pieties most people start spouting when they become religious. Just compare the sublime turbulence of Coltrane's later music to the violent idiocies of George W. Bush, who also uses the term spiritual awakening to describe a turning point in his life.

I wasn't a Coltrane fanatic. In fact, I had contempt for the widespread process of turning individual artists into celebrities. It seemed to me that when people like Coltrane became icons, the power of their music was partially replaced by the glamour of an image. Coltrane was only one of many compelling jazz musicians to emerge in the fifties and sixties, and I saw no point in turning any of these people into aesthetic legends. This would have been focusing on the wrong thing, missing the importance of the informal communities that formed around the musicians and their listeners. In the Age of Radio George Bush, these communities might have been the last pockets of artistic resistance, the last alternatives to a bullshit culture that was only getting worse.

In some ways, the Pequod crowd was one of these communities. They refused to let corporate America set the agenda for them. They put their own ideas, listening interests, and compositional practices ahead of the daily shit served up on the mainstream menu. If any of them had seen an issue of *Time*, *Newsweek*, or *The New York Times* in the past ten years, their conversation didn't show it. At times I thought this was insular and escapist, irresponsible. After all, I told myself, citizens of a country ought to pay close attention to current events and trends, especially in a democracy, which was based in theory on the informed consent of the governed. But I never raised this issue because I knew in advance what the answer would be, that the dominant information system in America was owned by the ruling class and functioned as disguised propaganda, transmitting not so much a message as a mood, an environment of images that encouraged people to get and spend as much as possible. I had heard this line of reasoning many times, at the Pequod and elsewhere, and though I felt it was basically true, I was tired of it. I just wanted to enjoy the music and books of my favorite composers and writers.

I wish I could say that the people at the café were among my favorite musicians. Certainly their dialogues intrigued me. But it troubled me that they never seemed to write or play any music. In fact, I got the impression that they felt it was more important to talk about music than to compose, perform, and listen to it. Perhaps they were turning aesthetic discourse into an art form, turning intelligent conversation into a form of civil disobedience, a refusal to become media zombies and compulsive consumers. Would there come a time when people could be arrested for refusing to watch TV and shop, choosing to talk about music instead?

When I pictured the police bursting in and closing the Pequod, pushing us out the door with guns and handcuffs, allowing the café to reopen only after TVs had been installed in every corner, I got a perverse thrill, a sense of being part of something larger than myself, even if the feeling was drenched in the pathos of a nation committing artistic suicide. Yes, I wanted to *hear* Coltrane and not just sit around talking about him. Yes, I had rejected the assumption that discourse on the universe could be replaced by a universe of discourse. But I also wanted to believe in the communities of conversational resistance that existed in small cafés all over the world. Would such communities prevent the president from declaring war on Afghanistan, Iraq, or other supposedly terrorist countries? Clearly not. But I thought at the time that they might be the only way to prevent the president from completing the work of his predecessors, *totally* reducing the nation to a state of terminal stupidity.

Was the pleasure I was getting from sitting by my window with a blanket—balanced between Coltrane and cold rain—also a form of resistance? I liked the idea quite a bit, since it meant I was being subversive without doing anything, simply by insisting on my own definition of pleasure, rather than subscribing to the mainstream's version of personal enjoyment. According to the mainstream, having fun would mean drinking beer and playing volleyball on the beach, laughing and smiling with well-built men and women. Or wearing a cowboy hat and riding a horse, looking tough and smoking a cigarette with mountains and a spectacular sunset in the background. Or beaming in a bar with beer foaming over the edge of a tall glass, a bear's head mounted above a mantelpiece in the background. Or driving a sports car through a redwood forest, hair blown back by wind and the ocean visible in the background.

Just thinking about these images made it hard to feel the power of Coltrane's music. I felt like a radio station slaughtered by sudden bursts of static. I wanted to smash my TV set. But since I didn't have one, I got up and walked out into the rain, which wasn't quite so nice when I was really getting wet. I walked for miles. I wasn't sure where I was going but I knew I had to get there. I passed through an old industrial neighborhood filled with abandoned factories and brick warehouses. Suddenly someone stepped out of one of the few residential buildings in the area, a decrepit three-story brownstone. He told me to come inside because he had something important to show me. I told myself not to follow him, that the situation might be dangerous, but I found myself going up the stairs with him anyway, all the way to a small room on the third floor. He offered me a cup of coffee, and we sat down at a small table by a window looking out over gabled housetops and water towers toward the blinking red lights of an oil refinery, and beyond that, toward the gliding lights of small boats in the harbor. We sat for two minutes without saying anything.

The silence made me uneasy. But even more unsettling was the distinct feeling that I wasn't in San Diego any longer. I knew that if I went outside it would still be San Diego, but what I saw from the window was clearly another time, another place. It looked like the early seventies in Baltimore, where I'd lived for about six months right after I graduated from college. I looked up into the face of my companion, hoping he would notice my confusion and tell me what was going on. But his face was blank, like a page right before it gets covered with words, or like a procession of somnambulists in long white gowns, moving along the edge of a cliff by the sea at four in the morning. I thought of a ladder made of wine, a chimpanzee with a book of crossword puzzles, a smooth piano solo forming a footbridge over a chasm. Then he pointed outside. About a hundred feet above the harbor, a light blue cube of light popped into the sky. It hovered for twenty-five seconds, then disappeared, taking a small chunk of space-time with it. I felt like the night was a camera taking my picture. Then it was two hours later. I was back on the street walking home.

I took my time. I always do my best thinking when I'm walking, and old industrial neighborhoods are perfect vehicles for moody ruminations. But something was preventing me from thinking, as if I could approach but not quite activate the verbal mechanisms that generate and sustain mental activity. If part of space-time had been removed, then apparently it was no longer possible to approach the world in quite the same way as before. I felt strangely unprotected, but also excited. When I looked at the silhouettes of factory smokestacks pressed against the dark sky, the broken warehouse windows, the garbage gusting in circles on potholed streets filled with shattered glass, they seemed to be parts of a musical score, a three-dimensional system of notation, a composition designed to be listened to so carefully that even when it was over the sound could still be heard, continuing beyond what would sound like silence to those not listening closely, leading its listeners far away from the noise built into their heads, down through smaller and smaller scales of perception, reaching the point beyond which nothing is and nothing isn't.

When I got home I sat in my favorite place by the window. I left the lights off and I didn't play any music. I felt no desire to turn on my computer, check e-mail, type out my impressions of the walk I'd just taken, or point and click my way through the maze of web sites. I wanted nothing more than to sit still and do nothing. I didn't even want a glass of water. It felt like I should have reached some kind of turning point in my life. But I didn't believe in turning points, or dramatic moments of any kind, since they seemed to occur only in movies and popular novels. I told myself that the next day would be the same as any other, that the real question was how to deal with unusual events that change nothing, have no obvious meaning, and don't even make a subtle difference that only becomes apparent years later.

I had no answer. But the next day Bob and I went to see a well-known mystic from Guatemala. Bob had been telling me about him for weeks, and though I'm not big on New Age celebrities, I thought it might be fun to see why Bob was so impressed. Strangely enough, the event was at a high school gym. The audience was arranged in a large semicircle that filled a basketball court. The mystic walked out from the men's locker room with no introduction, stood at the open end of the semicircle, smiled and put his hands together and bowed, then sat on a folding chair with his hands on his knees, eyes closed in concentration. We sat there in silence for maybe fifteen minutes. I didn't know what we were waiting for, but I didn't ask Bob for clarification because the silence seemed important, as if by listening to it carefully I would open myself to music arriving from an incomprehensible distance, sounds that would become music only because I was listening carefully, reducing the distance, or rather becoming the distance, containing it, becoming large enough to contain it without keeping it from expanding.

Something was happening. The air in the gym was congealing, like water becoming ice, collapsing into a large transparent sphere in front of the mystic. The sphere was slowly turning opaque and solid, hardening into a blue stone five times the size of a human head. The mystic opened his eyes, put his hands together and bowed to the stone, stood up and bowed to his audience, then turned and disappeared through the locker room door.

We sat there not knowing what to do. Finally a few people got up and touched the stone to make sure it was real. Soon everyone was inspecting it. It felt like any other stone I'd ever touched. What bothered me was the shape. It seemed too perfectly spherical to be real. But unless all of us had been hypnotized by the mystic into imagining the same thing, the stone was as real as anything else.

This was confirmed the next day when the San Diego morning paper reported that high school officials were confused about the appearance of a huge blue stone on their basketball court, and even more confused about how to remove it, since it was too large to fit through the gym doors. I sympathized with their problem. But I wasn't all that concerned about the stone. What mattered more to me was that the possibility of music, the silence I'd heard so distinctly the night before, had now become the reality of music, filling my body with sheets of sound, like light arriving from a distant star.

I didn't know if anyone else would have called it music, but I was more convinced than ever before that I had to keep my channels clear, keep Clear Channel out of my head, preserving the silence the music was emerging from. I wasn't sure how to live without noise in a country whose economic system relied on jingles and big-hit singles. But I knew I would spend the rest of my life developing my own compositional practice, my own system of notation, convinced that if I could find ways to write down what I was hearing, someone would someday figure out how to perform it.

A NEW KIND OF HAPPINESS

I don't remember who they were. But some time in the mid-1950s, when I was growing up on the south side of Chicago, three men, friends of my father I suppose, showed up at our house late one afternoon and did something I've never quite forgotten. After chatting pleasantly with my father for a few minutes, they asked him if they could make use of an old coffee table we kept in the corner of our living room. It was pushed up against a wall because one of its legs had been broken off. I'm not sure why we hadn't thrown it away. But one of the men insisted that it was perfect for their purposes. I dragged it into the center of the room. Then they pulled the shades and we all sat down on the floor with our hands about an inch above the table.

They told me that the table would soon be moving on its own, and sure enough, after a few minutes of weird silence, it began to shake, as if in the midst of an earthquake, even though no one was touching it and the floor was perfectly still. Thirty seconds later the shaking stopped, and one of the men addressed the table, speaking quite casually, as if he were talking to a friend, asking it to indicate the ages of everyone present. The table began tapping the floor, pausing at seven—my age at the time—and pausing, correctly, after much longer intervals for my father and the others. I sat there smiling, astonished. I couldn't think of anything to say. My father made some kind of joke and the men laughed. Then they went away.

I'm sure my father discussed the situation with me afterwards, but I don't recall what he said. All I know is that I was left with a mysterious feeling that has been with me all my life. I'm not religious, and I don't subscribe to any of the New Age attempts to account for "paranormal phenomena" like the one described above. Indeed, I think all existing pictures of the universe are inaccurate, misguided, and ultimately boring. History shows that people seem to need interpretations and will do almost anything to explain what they don't understand. But why should we force the world to make sense if that's not what it makes?

Of course, these thoughts were not in my mind as a boy growing up in Chicago, and they weren't in my mind ten years later, my final year in high school, as I sat in French class tuning out the teacher, staring at the floor, where panels of light and shade were thrown by dusty venetian blinds. I loved the way those panels moved with even the slightest breeze, and I often became so immersed in that trembling motion that I forgot where I was. My hand would remain on the open page of my notebook, so it looked like I might be learning, but instead of taking notes I was making abstract sketches, without paying any attention to what I was drawing. But one time, about a week before graduation, I was startled to find that instead of the usual squares and cubes and pyramids, I'd actually made a detailed illustration, a cobbled street of old shops and brick apartment buildings, a picture so vividly rendered that I couldn't believe my own hand had produced it. Somehow I had even managed to capture the opposite side of the street, sketching its partial reflection in the shop fronts. Where had I learned to draw so well? Even with careful effort, I'd never before been able to produce such an accurate picture of a place. In fact, I'd never drawn a picture that looked like much of anything. I stared at the page, imagining that beneath or perhaps within its blank surface all the possible pictures in the world were waiting to happen, needing only the proper atmosphere to manifest themselves.

The bell rang, ending class. The teacher, Mr. Blanc, gave me a dirty look and told me and a guy named Gary, who'd been sitting on the other side of the room, to stay after class. He told us our lack of attention was insulting and unacceptable. He made us open our notebooks and show him our notes for the day. I was shocked when I saw that Gary's page was exactly the same as mine, the same carefully rendered cobbled street of shops and apartment buildings, the same opposite side of the street reflected in the shop-front windows. At first Mr. Blanc was merely annoyed. But when he thought about the exact replication, he wanted an explanation. Gary and I just stood there looking stupid, shrugging repeatedly, truthfully insisting that we barely knew each other. Had we seen the same picture somewhere and by coincidence copied it into our notebooks at exactly the same time? We both said no, that we'd never seen such a picture and had never been to a place with a cobbled street. Mr. Blanc shook his head, stared out the window for a minute, then gave us extra homework, even though graduation was only a week away and none the other teachers were assigning any homework at all.

I assumed that Gary shared my amazement and would want to discuss the situation after Mr. Blanc dismissed us. But once we left the room and began walking down the corridor, he seemed annoyed when I started asking questions. Aside from telling me that he'd never seriously tried to draw anything, he did little more than shrug, nod, and shake his head. Then he said he was late for baseball practice and hurried away. We graduated the following week and never met again.

But in college I met many people who were fascinated by the story and had similar stories to tell. One story led to another, one person led to another, and six years later, through a series of friends and connections, I was living in a spiritual commune in Baltimore, one of many that began to appear all over the world in the late sixties. One day I was walking through an unfamiliar section of the city. I'm not sure where I was going, though I must have known at the time. After turning a number of corners, I realized I was lost, and with each attempt at retracing my steps I became even more unsure of where I was. To make things worse, it was getting dark, and the warehouses and factories that filled the neighborhood looked like cardboard props, flattened in silhouette against the deepening red of the winter sky.

Suddenly someone stepped out of one of the few residential buildings in the area, a decrepit three-story brownstone. Before I could ask him where I was, he told me to come inside because he had something important to show me. I told myself not to follow him, that the situation might be dangerous, but I found myself going up the stairs with him anyway, all the way to a small room on the third floor. He offered me a cup of coffee, and we sat down at a small table by a window looking out over gabled housetops and water towers toward the blinking red lights of an oil refinery, and beyond that, toward the gliding lights of small boats in the harbor. We sat there for two minutes without saying anything. There may have been jazz playing faintly in the background, perhaps from the room below or perhaps from the street, John Coltrane's *A Love Supreme*, though at the time I didn't know enough about jazz to identify what I was hearing. But that didn't stop me from listening to it so carefully that the sound of my companion's voice was jarring and intrusive, like a raging unicorn stomping through a meadow of human bones.

He said he'd been expecting me for a long time. When I asked him to explain, he got up and took a large envelope from the top drawer of a desk across the room. Inside was a folded map that he placed on the table in the fading light, opening it carefully. I wasn't sure what I was looking at, and he seemed surprised that I wasn't reacting with joy and astonishment. It occurred to me that I'd better try to simulate the response I assumed he was looking for, so I nodded slowly and gave him a faint but knowing smile. He nodded slowly and gave me a faint but knowing smile.

Two minutes later I was back on the street, the map was back in the envelope, tucked under my arm, and I was lost again, wandering through dark industrial streets that seemed to lead nowhere. Yet now that I had the map, the feeling of being lost was not unpleasant, as if the mere presence of a chart was enough to make the unknown landscape less threatening. It apparently made no difference that the map had nothing to do with Baltimore, that it seemed to have been drawn thousands of years before Baltimore even existed. All that mattered was the evidence that the human mind could transform three-dimensional space into a two-dimensional diagram, that the chaos and complexity of experience could be redesigned as an elegant abstraction, something so carefully drawn that it might have been a work of art. I began to enjoy not knowing where I was, immersing myself in the dismal brick structures I was surrounded by, the silhouettes of factory smokestacks, the crescent moonlight smeared on cracked and grimy windows, the occasional sounds of traffic in the distance.

When I finally got back to the commune house a few hours before dawn, the others were fascinated by the map. They seemed to understand exactly what they were looking at, talking in hushed reverential tones. I would have asked for an explanation, but I was desperately tired and quickly fell asleep. When I woke several hours later and asked about the map, no one seemed to know what I was talking about. I would have been more assertive in demanding an explanation, but I was afraid they might think I was crazy, so I let the matter drop. Three weeks later, someone found out that the leader of the commune had CIA connections, and I got away from that place as fast as I could. Thinking back on it now, I'm embarrassed that I didn't more quickly see the connection between the authoritarian qualities of our leader—he insisted on being called Master—and the crypto-fascism that the CIA is known for.

Today I assume that any group that operates with a hierarchical structure needs to be challenged or avoided. But at the time I was open to just about anything that promised an encounter with the unknowable, or at least with the unknown. Though I see now that I was looking for it in the wrong place, the fact remains that by making an honest mistake I set myself up for at least one strange experience I would have otherwise missed out on. In my bleaker moments, I tell myself that the commune was a waste of time, that I should have learned at the time to start shaping my life more productively. But even if the experience was in fact unnecessary, changing nothing leading nowhere, does that make it meaningless?

This question triggered a fierce debate at a Halloween party several years later. Heavily drunk, I told a guy dressed as a pirate that the most important things are the ones we can't interpret or classify. He told me that such an attitude was a clear sign of a weak and lazy mind. A long argument followed, and I ended up sober and depressed, feeling as if he'd made me look like a fool in front a girl I was trying to impress. But three days later I heard that he'd been struck by lightning. I took this as confirmation that my point of view was correct, that we should value most highly those events we can't readily grasp and place in a meaningful context.

This reminds me of someone I met soon after I left the commune, a guy selling his own specially prepared cough medicine. I never tried it, but I did experiment with a diet he proposed, living solely on peanuts and milk for six months. I don't recall the results, but I do recall that this man—I'll

call him Andy—may have been the only person I ever met
who routinely said upbeat things even though he was chroni-
cally depressed. It was unnerving. So unnerving, in fact, that
I wasn't entirely surprised when one day in late March 1973,
I found him in a sinister predicament.

I was taking a walk in the wooded park near the apartment I was living in, when I heard mean laughter coming
from a shady willow grove beside a river. Turning off the
path to investigate, I saw people scattering. Then I saw Andy
staggering in circles, barely able to stand. I called to him but
he seemed unaware of my presence, even when I was only
thirty feet away. I noticed that a circle had been drawn with
lime in the grass around him, and that—for reasons I still
don't understand—I was unable to enter that circle, just as
Andy was unable to leave it. For the next fifteen minutes I
tried to get his attention, yelling and gesturing. But he just
kept staggering in circles, waving his arms like a wounded
bird, convulsively shaking his head. I tried many times to
enter the circle. But something kept stopping me from taking
another step, though I knew there was nothing there, not
even a force field of the kind you might see in a science-fiction movie.

It was only by accident that the problem was resolved.
On my final attempt to penetrate the circle, I slipped on the
lime and erased a small segment. Suddenly Andy was fine.
He stood up straight, the blurred look disappeared from
his eyes, and he called to me in surprise, not sure why we
were there. Both of us crossed the boundary of the broken
circle without effort. He had no idea what was going on.
He knew only that earlier in the day he had overheard four
young men in a coffee shop discussing a battered book on

the table between them. When he asked them about it, they were more than willing to include him in their conversation, which was focused on magic and other demonic arts, though the young men were firm in their rejection of the term *demonic*, insisting that magic and related practices were only demonic from a Christian point of view, and had actually been significant agents of human evolution thousands of years before the teachings of Christ. When Andy equated magic with the stage performers who pass themselves off as magicians today, the young men insisted on giving him a demonstration. The last thing Andy remembered was leaving the coffee shop and walking into the park, and then a series of dissolving impressions, each seeming to exist only to be replaced by something else. When I told him what I'd seen he became disturbed, hostile and defensive, and finally stormed off in disgust. I never saw him again. But the partial circle was there on the grass in the park, no question about it. I confirmed its existence by showing it to my wife, though I never told her anything about it, not wanting her to think I was crazy.

Unfortunately, I'd already given her many reasons to think I was crazy, and she left me within a year, viciously humiliating me in front of my friends at a party, telling me that my strong opposition to the Vietnam War was stupid, throwing a drink in my face and storming out into a blizzard. The next time we met was in San Francisco ten years later. I was rushing down a street to meet a friend at the Museum of Modern Art when I saw a woman sitting on the sidewalk, her back against a garbage can, her trembling hand reaching out. I gave her a dollar bill, and as I hurried past, late for my appointment, it struck me that I knew her from somewhere.

I didn't want to look back, but the memory of her dirty face and matted hair kept returning throughout the day. I often think I know people from somewhere else, though in most cases I'm wrong. But this time I was right in a chilling way. I was just about to sit down in a café near the bay when the recollection came into focus, and I realized that the person whose face I couldn't forget was my former wife.

I rushed back to the place I'd seen her before, but she was gone. I waited two hours, until the sun went down, but she didn't come back. I kept returning throughout the week—indeed, throughout the next few months—with no success. I probably would have kept going back from time to time, had I not finally realized that the place itself was responsible for what I now recognize as a substitute perception. For those unfamiliar with this term, let me briefly explain. The Doctrine of Substitute Perceptions has its roots in modern theoretical physics, which postulates that the universe on its most basic levels is an ongoing fluctuation between everything that is and everything that isn't. We know nothing of the latter, but when we're extremely disturbed, or when the light and sound and smell and motion of a given place and time seem filled with undefined memories, we often catch an accidental glimpse of what doesn't exist. Since we have no words for what we're seeing in these moments, we translate them into something we do have words for, into substitute perceptions, things that might exist but probably don't.

Of course, the words we use to think about such perceptions alter them slightly, and this creates an uncertainty which forces us to consider the distortions our verbal capacities unavoidably produce, and even these speculations are dubious, caught in the same instability they've been driven to investigate, replicating and magnifying it, often beyond recognition, moving us further and further from the original substitution, until they have roughly the same connection to what they're addressing as the outermost ripples in a pond have to the pebble that produced them. Nothing is more important at this point in human history than the production of verbal strategies that can reverse the flow of distortion, running the film backwards from the final fading ripples to the pebble striking the surface of the pond, and beyond that, moving the pebble back into the hand of the person who tossed it, back through the neural connections in his arm and shoulder and then up into his head, where electrochemical motions and reverberations more numerous and complex than the drift of galaxies take place every second, mirrored by an undefinable substance that destroys anything that could possibly be compared to it.

Of course, we can be certain that many things *have* been compared to it, that many things *have* been destroyed, and no complete picture of the universe is possible unless all of these things can be recovered. There are two ways to approach this situation. We can either accept that parts of the universe are missing, which means that we also have to accept that the human quest for knowledge is doomed from the start, or we can take the more ambitious approach and try to make what's missing reappear. This might be as simple as squeezing a sponge, releasing what's been absorbed. Or it might be more like vomiting, pissing, or taking a shit, where what gets recovered has been transformed, leaving us to speculate on what it was before.

On what basis could such speculation even begin? On what basis, for example, could I convince myself that a cobbled street of shop fronts was once a pine on a ridge at sunset? How could such a statement be tested, scientifically confirmed? And why a *pine* on a ridge at sunset? Why not an oak or a maple? I wish my answer were more scientific. But like so many supposedly objective judgments, mine is influenced by a personal concern: I associate pines with survival, a connection I began making after a narrow escape from death.

Soon after I got my doctorate in anthropology, I took a trip to the Caucasus Mountains west of the Caspian Sea, partly for pleasure, partly to view the peak on which Prometheus was tortured, and partly because I wanted to do research on the descendents of a cult of magicians who supposedly inhabited the region three thousand years ago. Let me clarify: I had no intention of doing actual research. Instead, I wanted to prove that research is impossible, that anthropological research, for example, is based on the illusion that someone who is not part of a culture can understand that culture fully enough to make authoritative statements about it. The people I was planning to interview and observe had never been studied before. Though they had a very rich history going back thousands of years, they had yet to become parts of the official narrative called human knowledge. I had no desire to make them objects of study. Rather, my interactions with them would be the material used to demonstrate that people can't study others in a scientific sense, that the assumption you make when you decide to study anyone but yourself is arrogant and offensive. Back then I was convinced that I would soon be revolutionizing and even destroying the field of cultural anthropology. But my journey into the mountains took an unexpected turn.

About five days into the Caucasus, my guide and translator were killed in a rockslide. I was lucky to survive without
a scratch, but I saw no reason to count my blessings, since I
didn't know precisely where I was and all our food had been
buried in the avalanche. I wandered for several days, nearly
freezing to death at night and not sure if I was even heading in
the right direction, back toward civilization. I spent one night
in a cave, where I had to make a fire by rubbing two sticks
together. I spent the next night in the ruins of a chapel, where
the broken stained glass windows were jagged enough to cut
the shadows and make them bleed. I spent the next night in a
forest of demons, vaguely human shapes trembling in and out
of existence, biting my arms and legs, growling and laughing.
On the fourth day I came to a small community of people
living in stone huts. I assumed they were none other than the
group I'd come to the Caucasus to "study," but I couldn't be
sure, since my guide and translator were dead. Through a
series of awkward signs, I was finally able to tell them I was
lost and hungry, and they took me to a glade on the outskirts
of their community, where an old man was sitting placidly
under a pine so large it felt like the birthplace of all shadows.
Then they left the two of us alone, and we sat in silence.

At first, I felt scared and awkward. Then it occurred
to me that the old man was reading my thoughts, or rather,
plucking thoughts out of my head like someone plucking
small reptiles from a terrarium with tweezers. Each time he
removed a thought, I felt like I was eating a delicious meal.
Soon I felt so full I couldn't take another bite. But I kept ac-
cepting food because it wasn't food anymore. It was more like
a map, guiding me to a path leading out of the mountains.
I got up and started walking. I traveled through an exquisite

combination of mountain vistas and pines iridescent with sunlight, easily finding my way to a large town five miles from the Caspian Sea. I knew I'd been saved by magic. But part of me had been removed. I had no desire to do any more anthropology, subversive or otherwise.

In fact, I had no desire to do anything in particular, even when I got back to the States, where all my wise friends and loving relatives had great ideas about my future. I listened politely. But instead of trying to figure things out, I avoided plans and commitments as much as I could, working as little as possible, letting the spirit of improvisation guide me. One day I found myself in a café, randomly reading passages from an out-of-print book on avant-garde jazz, when I saw some-one reading the same book at a nearby table. We talked for hours, learning that our lives had been almost identical, filled with the same events and the same responses. But there was one crucial difference. Although we were both living in the spirit of improvisation, I was making sure that I didn't start thinking of it abstractly. I had no interest in developing a sys-tematic philosophy based on what I was doing. My friend, on the other hand, felt that everyone should lead a spontaneous life and that it was his job to make sure that random behavior soon became the norm, insisting that such a transformation could only take place if the principles of improvisation were carefully shaped into a doctrine. The more we talked, the more I became convinced that he was right, and the more I became convinced that he and I were almost identical in appearance, something that hadn't occurred to me until my opinions began to look like his.

I was just about to suggest that we should start meeting every day, but I caught myself before I said anything, realizing that such a proposal would interfere with the random quality of what we were trying to do. We parted without making plans. But over the next few months, we accidentally met on a regular basis, and out of our lengthy conversations the outlines of an improvisational system began to form. By the end of the year, I'd begun to see in a highly expanded way, noting differences between the ordinary person I'd been before and the expanded person I was slowly becoming. Of course, to summarize this difference with abstract generalizations would be to falsify its most basic assumption, turning a field of evolving possibilities into the kind of formulaic nonsense that the world's religions have made famous. Nonetheless, it's fair to say that where the ordinary person would see a museum, the expanded person would see new constellations. Where the ordinary person would see a dark blue raincoat, the expanded person would see an old man sleeping in a boat. Where the ordinary person would see a postcard of an alpine lake, the expanded person would see French windows with tossing drapes, then lightning bolts above Baffin Bay, then a house carried off in a flood, a human skull in a dusty attic, footsteps on a creaking floor approaching someone's bedroom, handcuffs on a window sill, a town of rusting robots. Where the ordinary person would see an urban skyline with mountains in the background, the expanded person would see piles of pages filled with obscure scientific notation caught by sudden wind and scattered in every direction, each page becoming a bird of prey sweeping over nearby fields, dropping suddenly and rising after a brief struggle with a rodent squirming in its talons, circling into a sunset filled with clouds in the shape of the Caspian Sea, others taking the shape of the Baltic Sea, or the Indian Ocean. Where the ordinary person would see a bee on a lime-green petal, the expanded person would see the White House caught in beams of dark light shooting down from cracks in a clear afternoon sky, the sound of shattering windows, the screams of terrified bureaucrats and politicians, the entire building suddenly reduced to the size of a doghouse, ripped from its foundations, sucked up into a crack in the sky with the sound of a zipper closing. Where the ordinary person would see someone forgetting to zip his fly, the expanded person would see someone forgetting to zip his fly.

The final comparison is clearly problematic—but not because it's inconsistent with what precedes it. In fact, this inconsistency is quite consistent with the improvisational perspective my friend and I were trying to cultivate. And this is precisely the problem: If there's always a difference between ordinary and expanded states of mind, then a pattern begins to form, and we need inconsistencies to break that pattern, leaving room for what can't be foreseen. But once we stipulate that inconsistencies will occur at irregular intervals, interfering with the pattern of differences, this too creates a pattern, an expectation that interruptions will occur, and irregularity itself becomes predictable.

It took me another year to see this clearly. But once I was able to put this disturbing insight into words, I stopped running into my friend, though I told myself that I still looked like his twin, and got a strange feeling whenever I looked at myself in the mirror, as if that flat glass reflection had somehow taken over. It was precisely to avoid this feeling that I started planning my life again, even to the point of getting a nine-to-five job with an overly serious boss and inflexible deadlines. I also began to avoid mirrors, looking at myself only in bodies of water, in ponds and lakes and puddles, where my image came back to me in slightly distorted form, altered by motions in the water, and by the presence of authentic non-reflexive depth beneath the liquid surface. Slowly I learned to live without the feeling of being replicated in flat planes of glass, releasing myself from the tyranny of artificial reflections.

Before I continue, let me briefly explain that my use of the word *twin* in the previous paragraph should not be taken symbolically, as if my friend were just a projection of my psychological perspective. He was definitely a separate person, and the cafés where our meetings occurred were not mere textual settings for a series of philosophical dialogues, but actual places, with lots of other customers occupying themselves in ways that had nothing to do with our discussions. There were people laughing, scowling, nodding, arguing, reading, coughing, burping, writing, whispering, farting, sneezing, drooling, scratching, kissing, staring, sucking, snoozing, shouting, snapping, doodling, squinting, fidgeting, slurping, cheering, snarling, winking, raving, wallowing, musing, eating, drinking, and doing anything else that people in cafés do. In fact, they were doing so many different things in so many different ways that it would be impossible to describe just one second of what was happening there, let alone describe the changes that took place from one moment to the next, accumulating relentlessly as the seconds, minutes, and hours passed, a massive unfolding that taken as a whole could be described as an improvisation, even if each individual had a fairly definite notion of what he or she was doing there. Had we really wanted to see what improvisation was, we could have just observed our surroundings. But we

were too absorbed in our planned improvisations, too identi-
fied with our own perspectives to see that the other people in
the cafés were not mere background presences in a narrative
that featured us as philosophical protagonists.

I don't mean to give the impression that I was mesmerized by the so-called grandeur of my own ego. If anything,
my problem has always been that I have little confidence in
myself, only a sporadic ability to respect my own perceptions.
The truth is that I rarely feel like a protagonist, even in the
story I keep telling myself about myself, and certainly back
then I felt even less entitled to take myself seriously.

This feeling was painfully present in the jobs I ended
up with. I always thought I was too good for the kind of work
I was capable of getting, and not good enough for the kind of
work I wanted. Though I had a Ph.D. in cultural anthropology, I never put much effort into finding an academic job because I was sure I wasn't smart enough to work and socialize
with brainy professors who had never seriously doubted their
intelligence or questioned their right to lecture at people. My
lack of confidence left me scrambling from one part-time job
to another, performing tasks that were so stupid I couldn't
take them seriously. In every case, I soon either quit or got
fired. But I did manage to find one job I liked. Ironically
enough, it was at the local university, though it didn't involve
teaching and trying to pretend to be someone's colleague.

I got the job by chance. I was visiting a friend, the only
professor I've ever met who doesn't scare me by trying to
be smart all the time. I picked up what looked like an old
bone on the desk of his study. It felt funny in my hands, as
if I could feel its age and origins. I closed my eyes and tried
to identify the sensation more precisely, but the motion of

words in my head, the tools with which I was trying to name the feeling, took the form of a car driving off a cliff, leaving me with nothing. The blank space was slowly replaced by a scene that had no connection to any place I'd ever been, though I somehow knew I was looking at a Stone Age village in southern France, a wounded man sitting in the shade of a willow grove by a river, carefully chipping one piece of rock with another.

I opened my eyes and looked at my friend, who was watching me with a puzzled expression. When I closed my eyes again the scene was gone. He asked if I was okay, and I told him what I'd felt and seen. His eyes were bright with amazement. He explained that the bone I'd picked up was actually a Stone Age tool from the Magdalenian period, and that one of his colleagues had found it in southern France during a recent excavation. He urged me to talk about the village I'd seen, and was excited when the fragmented description I provided matched the reconstructions he and other members of the Physical Anthropology Department had been able to create from existing evidence.

He gave me two other artifacts, both of which triggered similar sensations in my hands and gaps in my mental perceptions, followed by unfamiliar scenes. And both times, the places I described were consistent with the approved academic reconstructions, even though, having focused on modern anthropological theory as a graduate student, I knew almost nothing about Stone Age societies. This left me with an eerie feeling, but my friend was enthusiastic. Over the next few weeks, he was able to arrange a research position for me at the university. It was a great job. All I had to do was handle various artifacts and provide descriptions of the places and events I saw, working painstakingly with my friend, his colleagues, and their illustrators, gradually creating a series of detailed pictures of Late Paleolithic society. These drawings were subsequently published in the *Journal of Physical Anthropology* and created an international stir in the academic community. Meanwhile, I was making $50 an hour, and for once I was able to support myself by doing something I liked.

My Stone Age visions were accompanied by a pleasant mental sensation. Earlier I said it was like driving off a cliff. But as I grew more accustomed to the process, it was more like tumbling over a waterfall and plunging hundreds of feet into cool flashing water without getting hurt. The visions themselves lasted longer and longer, were increasingly vivid and detailed. In such moments, I felt I was really there, back in Paleolithic villages. I could feel the ground beneath my feet and began taking tentative steps, moving carefully through the prehistoric landscape. The space became more tangible, more sharply focused, more obviously different from the space I was used to. The absence of noise was unnerving at first. The Stone Age air was so clean I could hardly breathe it. But soon I developed a strong preference for ancient atmospheres, an attraction that verged on addiction. The toxic patterns of modern life became increasingly repulsive. I was bored unless I was in the past. But I couldn't completely escape the fear that at some point I might get stuck there.

About three months after the visions began, I reached a point of no return. My eyes actually met those of a young boy, sitting outside of a large hut made of the bones and skulls of mastodons. I was certain that he not only saw but also recognized me. To confirm this feeling, I asked my friend to let me work again with the hand ax that had triggered the vision, and precisely the same scene appeared. This time my sense of the place was so complete that I actually heard birds in the trees and felt rain approaching from the north. The boy looked up and met my eyes and smiled. He said something I didn't understand, but I knew I should follow him as he got up and walked along the riverbank.

Soon we were well beyond the edge of the village, following a trail through a dense forest. The smell of rain approaching grew stronger by the minute. There was thunder in the distance, wind in the treetops. Before too long, we reached a clearing, in the center of which was a pile of stones that seemed to be a sacrificial altar. Three men gripping sharp stone objects, knives apparently, approached from the other side of the clearing. I was taken by a fear so strong that everything went blank, and I found myself on the floor of my friend's office, looking up into his concerned face, taking the glass of water he was putting in my hand. He told me I'd been in my usual trance when suddenly I began speaking, or rather moving my mouth in response to non-verbal sounds that seemed to be coming *through* me but not *from* me. When he'd asked me what I was seeing, I'd dropped the axe and slumped down out of my chair onto the floor. We both agreed I'd seen enough for one day.

From that point on, the artifacts they gave me had no effect. The visions were gone. But I didn't want to lose the job, so I began making things up, basing my invented visions on previous experiences and altering them slightly to keep things interesting. This went on for a month, resulting in several vivid reconstructions. But finally I made a bad mistake, reporting that the women in a village I was visiting had elaborate hairstyles. The professor I was working with at the time looked surprised but said nothing, faithfully jotting down my observation.

Two days later, my friend angrily told me over the phone that I'd been dismissed, that the pictures I'd been giving them over the past two weeks had seemed increasingly improbable, and that the notion of Paleolithic women with fancy hairdos was an obvious fabrication. The fact that I was making things up had thrown all my work into question, and a few of his colleagues were even thinking of suing me for wasting their time and compromising their reputations with a cynical hoax. I packed my bags and left town the next day. I had no further contact with my friend. But I was pleasantly shocked one day to find an article in the *Journal of Physical Anthropology* indicating that statues of Magdalenian women with ornate coiffures had recently been discovered.

Two years and five jobs later, I was in northern California working as a forest ranger. After all the idiotic things I'd had to do to survive, I was finally doing something I liked again. Though the job was boring at times, I loved the weather patterns in that part of California, the cold wind and the rain that came so frequently, the absence of noise that reminded me of the prehistoric world I could no longer visit. On just such a day, I was walking in the darkest depth of the forest with Ben, a fellow ranger, performing one of our daily tasks. Suddenly, behind a huge rock, we found a monstrous egg with what sounded like a gigantic baby bird inside, savagely smashing the shell with its beak. We weren't sure what to do. The wind increased, bending the trees and howling, making a sound that almost drowned out the cries of the unborn bird. Finally I picked up a rock and smashed the egg. It made a sound like wind chimes as it shattered. Inside was an egg of normal size, cracked slightly. But when Ben tried to lift the egg it shattered, and what remained of the bird inside indicated that it had been dead for several days.

We quickly confirmed that we'd seen and heard the same thing, that the huge egg and monstrous cries had not been imagined. We decided not to file a report, not wanting to be accused of collaborating in a hoax. But since neither of us could get the incident out of our minds, two days later we met in a nearby town for dinner and tried to reason things out. Though we came up with several entertaining theories, we left the restaurant just as confused as we were before. I thought of the Doctrine of Substitute Perceptions, but quickly dismissed it, since I didn't see how two people could substitute exactly the same perception.

As we walked away from the restaurant and strolled along the town's pleasant waterfront, we noticed a group of people in front of us, talking loudly in a language I didn't recognize, apparently drunk. Suddenly one of them pulled out an umbrella, which was odd, since the night was unusually clear, with no threat of rain. After thrusting it up at the sky a few times, she spun around and faced us with a smile, swinging it in wide arcs, as if to enclose us in an invisible circle. Then she threw it down at our feet.

Ben and I stood there confused and amazed, staring at the umbrella. I thought I could hear carnival music in the distance, happy voices playing games and laughing. The umbrella began to flicker, like a lantern flame about to go out. It emitted an odd, crackling sound, similar to the sound of cellophane being crumpled, and in a dazzling array of multi-colored light, its ends curled up, its color changed, and it briefly became a flaming bird rising out of its own ashes. Then it was simply a broken egg on the pavement.

I looked up, expecting to meet the eyes of the strange woman and demand an explanation. But she and her friends were getting into a car on the corner, closing the doors and driving away. I turned to Ben, who agreed with me that everything had happened as I described it above. The only difference was that he compared the crackling sound of the umbrella to strips of bacon frying in a skillet, which made me mentally revise my description several times, thinking that the umbrella sounded like static on a radio, like a popped balloon spiraling unpredictably through a bedroom and shooting out the window, like velcro in a microphone, like a body very slowly drawn and quartered.

When we later wrote down our descriptions, I went back to the simile of crumpled cellophane, and Ben described it that way too, explaining that I'd clearly come up with a more accurate comparison, and that the only reason he'd initially thought of bacon was that we'd seen a broken egg on the pavement. This led me to think about why I tend to be so influenced by the perceptions and needs of others, why I'll do anything to please, becoming a very carefully edited version of myself. I started getting anxious that Ben might use our shared experience to get to know me better. I knew that if we became close friends I would soon start changing myself in self-degrading ways, so I quit my job and moved away, becoming an unfamiliar face in an unfamiliar city.

An extreme reaction? I knew of course that it was. I ridiculed myself for nearly a month, accusing myself of

cowardice, of becoming a hermit with no religious justifi-
cation. But I also knew that what I'd done was consistent
with my psychological needs at the time, even if most people
would say that meaningful human interaction is psychologi-
cally necessary for anyone trying to confront the mysteries
of existence. But as I grew older I had less and less tolerance
for the annoying complexities people always confronted me
with. Even though Ben and I had communicated pleasantly
and clearly when discussing our strange experience, I knew
that if we got to know each other better we would begin
to get on each other's nerves, and I'd reached this point so
many times in the past that I saw no reason to repeat the
pattern. Yes, I was withdrawing from a crucial aspect of life.
But I saw no alternative. I wanted as little noise in my head
as possible.

About a year later, I inherited a big sum of money
from a childless aunt who had always thought of me as her
son. This allowed me to quit my latest idiotic job and move
to a nice apartment facing a park with a view of the city's
waterfront in the distance. Most people in a similar situation
would probably have spent the money on a fancy car or traveled around the world, but I preferred to pass long parts of
each day staring out the window, fascinated by how much
there was to see. The more I looked, the more I saw. The
more I saw, the more I looked. The slow but steady process
of expansion was delicious. But then something happened
that forced me to learn to appreciate my limits.

I'd gone out at sundown and walked well into the night,
down many familiar streets of shops and pointed housetops.
Around midnight, I reached a familiar intersection where in
the past I'd always turned right, the first step in returning to

my apartment. This time I turned left, wanting to expand the boundaries of my wandering. I was quickly surprised. This part of the street was cobbled, unlike the part of the street I was familiar with. The buildings were old but well-preserved, a combination of small shops, brownstones, and two-story brick houses. I enjoyed looking at them so much that I felt stupid for having avoided this part of the street before, and I reminded myself about the dangers of habit, the exclusions that result when you do the same things all the time. I loved the way the moonlight spread on the wet cobbles, the way the shops became phantom reflections in the windows on the other side of the street. But the crescent moon went behind the clouds, and everything vanished, leaving only the sidewalk and a wooden bench. I thought of going back to the intersection, but it wasn't there anymore, so I sat on the bench and waited, looking at nothing.

In fact, it was less than nothing. Instead of leaving an open space, the buildings had disappeared so fully that even their absence had vanished. At first I found this unnerving. But as I began to accept it, the absence of anything, the absence even of absence, began to seem quite remarkable, like a prerequisite for a new kind of happiness. I had always assumed that the absence of absence would mean presence. But this was not the case. What I felt instead was an absence that was no longer merely the opposite of presence, but rather its precondition, its origin, its point of departure. I felt privileged to be in its presence, or rather its absence, and I wanted to think that this indefinable moment, which could only be described by saying what it wasn't, was somehow deserved, that my willingness to live without any definite purpose, existing only to witness the present moment unfolding, had made me worthy of an experience reserved for mystics after long years of rigorous discipline. I started laughing, dissolving the fear that for decades had pushed me to believe that I was nothing unless I could present myself to the world as a conscious coherent being.

Unfortunately, the clouds finally dispersed. The crescent moon reappeared, bringing back the cobbled street of old buildings, and with it the intersection, about a hundred feet to my right. The bench I'd been sitting on was gone. There was nothing to do but return to the life I knew. Obviously, I wasn't going back to a terrible existence. In some ways, it was what I'd always wanted—a beautiful apartment in a city I liked with no financial pressures. But now things weren't the same. Compared to what I'd been feeling in the dark, my normal sense of myself and the world was a keen disappointment. I had to deal with months of stiff depression before I started to feel that everyday life was acceptable again.

The turning point in my recovery came when I learned to adjust my venetian blinds. I don't mean that I didn't know how to do it before, just that for the first time I was doing it for a purpose other than comfort, filling my apartment's broad oak floorboards with a pattern of light and shade so exquisitely detailed that I could observe it like an evolving work of art, carefully tracking its transformations throughout the day. Of course I couldn't paraphrase what I was looking at, any more than I could paraphrase an abstract painting. So instead of treating the changing patterns on my floor as if they were parts of a code I could crack, I tried to explain to myself why interpretation was impossible.

I came up with all sorts of stupid ideas, and I'm glad I was wise enough to reject them one by one. I won't say I didn't take some of them too seriously for a day or some-times even a week, and I won't say that I didn't enjoy the often absurdly complex process of creating them. Explaining why something can't be explained can be entertaining. But I wanted to think I was doing more than jerking off in my head. I somehow knew that what I was looking for would simply arrive one day on its own, seeming to come out of nowhere, though in fact it would have been assembling itself quietly for a long time, waiting until I'd cleared the noise from my head.

The more I looked at the light and shade on the floor, the more I thought it was made of water, and though I knew this wasn't strictly true, the feeling it gave me seemed to relax my depression, letting it rise out of me like steam from coffee. If I was reading water, what was it telling me? Or rather, why was it impossible to know what it was telling me? I thought about the mind of water, an ancient form of molecular intel-ligence that had transformed the planet billions of years ago, setting the stage for everything that followed. I was mostly water. My interpreting brain was mostly water. By meditat-ing on water, I could look at what I was made of.

I considered moving to an apartment closer to the waterfront, giving myself direct access to the source. But I reminded myself that it wasn't really water on my floor. It was light, and light was older than water, preceding it by billions of years in the evolution of the universe. Light in itself was far too vast, far too fast, for human understand-ing. But viewing the light as water, I could bring it closer to home, closer to my body, my biochemical map, watch-ing it on my floor contained in a panel shaped like a page, with a language of shadows that moved in the breeze, as if

I were looking at words trembling on a page of water. Yet
the words I used when I spoke or thought were not made of
water, and they had no way of explaining what the mind of
water was. Language, of course, was the only way I could
tell myself what I knew. Yet once I told myself what I knew,
I was trapped in a verbal reduction, a grammatical picture
of something that was not the thing itself, something like the
difference between a fishbowl and the sea.

But if words were the enemy, why were they inform-
ing on themselves, encouraging me to perceive without
language? Were there other kinds of language that words
were just an imprecise translation of? Could a lifetime of
watching the shifting pattern on my floor somehow teach me
to read the language of water, the language I was made of,
and also teach me to read the language of light, the language
of eternity, without corrupting them with words? There was
only one way to find out.

WORLDS CONVERGING

I recently read in a magazine that it's not unusual for a couple to spend more than $3000 on a high school prom. I can't say I was surprised. Over the years, I've become thoroughly accustomed to the materialistic stupidity of mainstream America. But I can't imagine spending even a penny to go to a prom. During my high school years, I never went to a prom and never wanted to. I was nervous around women, uncomfortable wearing formal outfits, and scared of large gatherings governed by rigid codes of conduct. At one point, though, I was pressured. A few days before one of the proms, there were several girls in my class who didn't have dates, and it was widely assumed back then that it was deeply humiliating, tragic in fact, for a girl not to go to a prom. So someone called my mother and begged her to get me to call one of these unfortunate girls—I'll call her Pam—and save her from a bad situation.

I was anxious and confused. It seemed to me that a girl receiving a forced phone call a few nights before the prom would be even more humiliated than if no one called. But my mother explained how painful it would be for Pam to have no date, how it would give her severe feelings of inferiority that might ruin the rest of her life. She convinced me that all I had to do was take her there, say a few nice things, and let her spend the rest of the night talking to her friends while I was talking to mine. My mother was great at making me feel sorry for others and even better at embarrassing me if I felt sorry for myself.

The call itself took less than a minute. It was clearly weird for both of us. When I got off the phone I was relieved and pleased with myself at first, but as I began to think about actually going to the prom I got scared. I imagined myself saying all the wrong things, trying to dance and stepping on Pam's feet, watching her roll her eyes and giggle with her friends, not trying very hard to conceal the fact that they were talking about me. My mother could read the tension in my face, and soon she decided that she'd gone too far, not respecting my limitations as a scared sixteen-year-old. She phoned Pam's mom and called the whole thing off.

I still remember how relieved I was. I'd been hating my face in the bathroom mirror, rehearsing what I might say to Pam the following night, when my mother knocked on the door and told me I didn't have to go. I suddenly felt like I was only reading the tragic story I'd been the protagonist of just a moment before. Yes, a truly painful story makes you feel the disturbance of its characters. But this isn't the same as being one of those characters. When I pulled my face away from the face that was hating me in the mirror, I felt like someone closing a book, leaving the characters and their conflicts behind. I spent the rest of the night staring out the window into the dark, so happy and relaxed that I didn't even need to distract myself by listening to my favorite songs on the radio.

I soon found out that someone else had taken Pam to the prom. Several years later, a friend told me that in college she became a campus sensation, dating and fucking everyone. An alumni newsletter I looked at maybe ten years ago reported that Pam had married an investment banker and was dividing her time between Beverly Hills and the French Riviera. So apparently my failure that night had no lasting effect. But my recollection of the situation has led me to consider two important aspects of social life for young men and women: dating and parties. I think most people have positive feelings when they first hear these words. But in their most honest moments, they will probably realize that their actual experiences with dates and parties have often been difficult, embarrassing, and boring. So why are these activities seen in a positive light? Why don't people find better ways to socialize?

First, let me explain that I'm not a loner. I've never had any trouble meeting people and socializing. But over the last ten years, I've avoided dates and parties. I see no reason to subject myself to the expectations that accompany these activities. Before I got married three years ago, I had worked out a relaxed way of developing a relationship. When I wanted to get to know someone, I would begin a friendship, making daytime plans that didn't involve the trappings of a date. If the woman and I seemed to like each other over a period of time, we would start meeting at night, still thinking in terms of friendship. The atmosphere was always casual, free of expectations, at least on my side. As for parties, I would only accept invitations if most of the guests were already friends of mine, and only if the number of people attending was less than ten. I never understood why people looked forward to standing in a room full of strangers, acquaintances, and maybe a few friends, holding a clear plastic cup of wine and eating chunks of cheese off toothpicks, making small talk and repeatedly getting interrupted. How can you enjoy situations like this unless you're drunk?

I tried faking it for years, calling women up and making plans, showing up at large gatherings filled with deafening music, acting like I was more of a date-and-party person than I really was. But I always found casual socializing more fun than formal interactions. My first erotic encounter took place relatively late in life, when I was getting drunk with friends during my sophomore year in college. Bombed out of our minds at midnight, we decided to call some girls we knew from our history class and see if they wanted to go out for a drive. They said they did, so we picked them up and spent the next four hours kissing wildly in the car, caressing all the fun body parts, making all the erotic noises, though our clothes were on the entire time.

Later that same year, I actually got up the nerve to call one of these girls and go out with her sober. It was painfully awkward, nowhere near as much fun as being drunk and spontaneous. We went to see an Italian film called *Zabriskie Point*. One of my friends had raved about it a few weeks before, but my date and I agreed that the only good thing about it was the use of a Pink Floyd song to heighten the climactic scene in Death Valley. When I told her that Pink Floyd's first two albums had taken music in a whole new direction, she laughed and said that if I wanted to know what avant-garde music really was, I should listen to John Coltrane. I pretended to know who Coltrane was and disagreed with her, claiming that he was nothing compared to Pink Floyd.

I've never liked fighting with people, but in this case the argument seemed playful, even promising. She kept putting her hand on my arm, leading me to think that we might end up in bed. But on our way back to my dorm room, we ran into a friend who told us that we just *had* to come inside and hear an amazing piece of music. He took us up three flights to a small room filled with marijuana smoke. The same black-light poster appeared on the ceiling and all four walls, an adaptation of one of my favorite M. C. Escher engravings, with people going up and down stone flights of stairs that never connect, seeming to exist in parallel dimensions. The more dope we smoked, the more the Escher image mirrored the music, a jazz composition in four movements, each one framing and shaping the others, each one wildly graceful in ways I wasn't prepared for. I wasn't sure if I liked it at first, but halfway into the final movement, I knew my life would never be the same. Pink Floyd was nothing by comparison.

I assumed that my date was just as amazed as I was. She was leaning back on a pile of cushions, bobbing her head and smiling. Her eyes were closed and her hands were swaying like plants on the ocean floor. But after we left, she told me that the music sounded like something her parents might have enjoyed. She couldn't believe it excited me so much. I was going to defend my musical taste when she said she was tired and had to go home. The long walk across campus to her dorm was silent and painful, so I dropped her off without even trying to get a goodnight kiss, then went back to my friend's room to smoke more dope and hear the album again, wondering what it was. It turned out to be John Coltrane's *A Love Supreme*.

Eleven years later, the same album had a very different effect on a woman I was involved with, convincing her that we had to get married as soon as possible. Twenty-two years after that, *A Love Supreme* was playing on the radio when I found out that a former girlfriend had been killed when hijacked planes hit the World Trade Center. When patterns like this appear, it's easy to think that you're dealing with more than a coincidence, that whatever it is that keeps repeating itself is a message from the universe, a symbol that calls for careful interpretation. There's a lot I could say on the subject, but none of it would be anything more than conjecture, and besides, I don't want to lose track of what I was talking about before, the plight of the woman who never gets prom invitations, trying to believe the half-baked consolations of her well-intentioned parents, trying to appreciate the tact of her beautiful popular girlfriends, who make sure they don't talk about the fun they had at the prom when she's around.

I'm tempted to say that most teenage girls in this position are getting a taste of things to come, that they won't turn out like Pam with dates galore and wealthy husbands. I'm also tempted to say that some of these girls do even better than Pam, growing up to become famous models and Hollywood screen idols. But why speculate on such matters, which are too complex and uncertain for the kind of attention I'm likely to give them? I'd rather focus on the pain of the moment, bringing the story into the new millennium, introducing someone who isn't as fortunate as Pam—I'll call her Megan—a girl who doesn't get any last-minute phone calls.

She tells herself that proms are boring anyway, and besides, now she can stay home and watch that made-for-TV movie she's heard such good things about, the one in which a horny therapist remains true to his wife, even after she has a mastectomy, even though his young and sexy female clients keep trying to seduce him. But the movie turns out to be stupid. It isn't really about the integrity of the shrink, but about the cleavage of the clients, all of whom have apparently had first-class boob jobs, and this just makes Megan wish that her father was rich enough to pay for implants, and maybe also for a nose job.

So she flips through the channels until she finds a documentary on conspiracy theories, focusing especially on the events of 9/11, carefully showing that the Bush administration was aware of Al-Qaida's plans but chose to let the violence occur, making increased military spending and invasive security measures and restrictions seem quite reasonable to a scared and confused population. Megan finds this theory paranoid and repulsive, but somehow she can't quite rule it out, especially when it's combined with a theory claiming that Bush had conspired with Cheney prior to the 2000 elections, planning a war to devastate Iraq and establish U.S. military supremacy in the region, creating oil opportunities for Bush and business opportunities for Cheney and others like him. Did Bush and his staff ever truly believe that Saddam Hussein had weapons of mass destruction? Clearly not, the documentary insists, providing ample evidence. Again Megan is disgusted. But this time it's not so much the theory that disturbs her, but the fact that it makes good sense, especially when compared to the explanations the White House gave when no one could find any weapons of mass destruction after the war.

Megan tells herself that now she's glad she didn't go to the prom, since the documentary has given her something important to think about, while the prom would have been filled with bad music, fake laughter, and excessive glitter, signifying nothing. But when she brushes her teeth before going to bed, she doesn't like what she sees in the mirror, and she can't escape the suspicion that her interest in the documentary is only a pathetic escape from feelings of inferiority. She begins to hate herself again, but unlike the many moments of self-disgust she's had before, this one meets firm opposition—the shots of the Twin Towers burning, the shots of Baghdad burning. Her self-hatred merges with her hatred for the White House, resulting in something that bears no resemblance to the feelings that produced it, something unexpected, much in the same way that hydrogen and oxygen combine to become water, a substance that in no way resembles the elements that produced it. Of course, we're accustomed to water. But nothing can prepare us for what happens when two different kinds of hatred converge, like a face and its mirrored reflection hating each other for different reasons, like someone reading a story becoming the person he thought he was reading about, suddenly finding that his destination seems to be a library lost in a chasm deep in the Hindu Kush, stone walls cracked and covered with vines, books that make sense in every language, philosophical and scientific perspectives from an abandoned civilization.

Few people know that the place exists, and fewer still can tell him even roughly where it is. There's nothing he can do but follow dubious maps through towering mountains, knowing he's in the right place only after he gets sick of knowing he's in the wrong place. But he finally stands in snow, more than 10,000 feet high, looking down 3,000 feet into thick vegetation, a chasm briefly shining in midday sunlight.

Scanning carefully, his binoculars capture the stone towers of the library he's been looking for. But his elation is restrained, for he can see that getting down into that chasm would be hard even for an experienced climber. Three times in his descent he nearly dies, falling suddenly through fields of snow that weren't as firm as they looked, and when at last he reaches the magical building, he collapses and sleeps in its alabaster portico for more than a day, waking right before the sun disappears behind the mountains.

When he goes inside and acclimates his eyes to the dark, he finds that the books are made of water, or some substance that resembles water but requires no container to maintain a firm shape. Nothing prepared him for this, for inscriptions that float on trembling liquid surfaces and not on flat white paper. It occurs to him that books like this are designed to be imbibed, not examined with his eyes and mind, that once he's taken in what the pages contain, the words will be traveling in his blood, through tissues, muscles and bones, biochemically absorbed. Over time, this liquid wisdom will have given him a new physical vibration, something which will compel him into situations he would have previously avoided, forcing him to change, learning slowly through repeated confrontations what would have been only an abstract lesson before, when absorbed through the eyes and mind from paper pages.

The prospect of changing so thoroughly is unnerving, leading him to wonder why the people who produced these books abandoned them to the ravages of time, and the feeling of the present becoming the past is suddenly magnified. Something tells him to look out the window, which opens onto the motion of shadows across a lawn, two stopped-up stone fountains covered with dead leaves caught in gusts of cold wind, occasional bars of sunlight finding their way down into the chasm, filtered by a dense canopy of branches and leaves. He knows he's never been here before, but the feeling produced by the scene in the window briefly reminds him of hundreds of other windows, hundreds of other feelings conjured by looking out those windows, and each remembered window brings back hundreds of other feelings, hundreds of other windows, each becoming hundreds of other windows, and it's precisely this feeling that leads Megan to turn away from the mirror, escaping the face that looks back from the glass like a disappointed reader. She moves to her favorite place in the house, the window in her bedroom, leaving behind the brutal sensation of being too plain to be at the prom. She suddenly knows that it doesn't make any difference, that nothing makes any difference except for a place that she can't quite remember, the overpowering sensation that she's only where she is because she's also somewhere else, that she's only in her second-floor bedroom sitting by a window facing a dense canopy of branches, leaves, and moonlight because she's also looking out on thousands of other scenes through thousands of other windows.

A complete account of Megan's transformation would have to include a feminist analysis of her situation, focusing on what happens when a woman learns from a crisis that she doesn't need men to survive, that she can make it on her own, that social conventions like dates and proms and parties leave women in a painfully passive position. To get beyond this, some women go to the opposite extreme, becoming sexual predators, like a feminist I got to know a few years ago, an avant-garde composer in her late twenties who pursued and slept with as many men as possible, refusing to take any of them seriously because she didn't want the dreary complexities and frustrations that pass for intimacy in the early twenty-first century. But she didn't know that she had a carefully repressed Electra complex, so when one of her men resembled her father closely—and she didn't see the connection clearly enough to resist it—she became insanely possessive and wanted a long-term commitment, got pregnant on purpose, only to need therapy years later when she couldn't stand how tenderly her husband treated their daughter.

When problems get as complex as this one, it's clear that gender is no longer the primary issue. The problem is complexity itself. What does it mean to live in a world that not only manufactures complexity, but also forces or at least encourages people to lose themselves in their own complexities? A friend recently told me about two of his colleagues, anthropology professors who fell in love at an academic conference, unaware that under fake names and identities they'd already had great sex many times online. Because their computers were in separate parts of the large house they bought after getting married, they continued their Internet passion without suspecting anything. But their sex life in reality couldn't measure up to what they did in cyberspace, leading both to become so absorbed in virtual sex that they lost interest in each other as flesh and blood partners, and before too long they were filing for divorce.

Of course, the Internet isn't always a source of disaster. It doesn't have to become a labyrinth of blurred and distorted complexities. At times it offers crucial compensations, supplementary worlds that momentarily save us when the real world offers nothing but boredom, frustration, loneliness, and tragedy. Indeed, it's tempting to think that over the years Megan has developed a passionate life online, a network of digital partners who provide her with pleasures she might not have access to in any other way, or that she consoles herself on the night of the prom by visiting anti-prom chat rooms, learning that virtual sisterhood is just as powerful as any other kind. But the truth is that her parents have kept computers out of their household, convinced that the Internet is a tool of the Devil.

Megan goes to bed. Her sleep is magnificent. She wakes up the next day and buys a copy of *Das Kapital*, reads it carefully over the next five years, graduates *magna cum laude* from Stanford, gets a doctorate in political theory and becomes a widely-respected neo-Marxist professor at Harvard, publishing a book on the need for close government regulation of legal and health-care services, a text that inspires over a hundred million people to vote for a third-party candidate in the next presidential election, a socialist who lives up to campaign promises when he enters the White House, taxing the rich and big corporations heavily, taking a huge amount from the defense budget and putting it into environmental projects, waging war on financial inequality.

I know that some readers will probably find this ending unrealistic. If I wanted, I could show that no fiction can truly be realistic, that the distance between verbal and physical existence is greater than it seems. But if I'm too convincing in making this point, much of what I've written here will become unconvincing. Besides, I could also argue that there's nothing unrealistic about someone improving her life in response to a subtle change in her outlook. Happy endings aren't always mere Hollywood fantasies. For instance, I'm currently married to the most beautiful woman in the world, even though I grew up thinking that no girl I was attracted to would ever be attracted to me. If I wrote about this relationship in a complex work of fiction, would it be unrealistic? Would readers keep waiting for me to turn back into a pumpkin? Would they keep expecting a disturbing reversal, a sudden twist, a shattering moment of clarification? These are the things that most readers of serious fiction expect and even insist on, and they feel contempt if they don't get what they want, if they're forced to confront a different kind of ending.

Of course, no one wants to buy a book, spend hours reading it, and then feel cheated by the ending. It's too much like falling in love, developing marvelous expectations, moving in with your partner, only to find within two years that you can't stand each other. Fortunately, due to the wonders of modern science, such disappointments will soon be a thing of the past, at least in fiction. People familiar with twentieth-century physics will already know what I'm talking about: the so-called many-worlds interpretation of quantum mechanics. Our normal view of the world is that when something happens, other things don't. For instance, when Megan grows up to become a famous neo-Marxist professor at Harvard, she doesn't also become a cocktail waitress trapped in a frustrating marriage. But according to the many-worlds approach to quantum physics, all things that could happen do. In the universe we're accustomed to, Megan's book triggers a major change in American politics. In a parallel universe, which functions just like ours but includes events that don't happen here, Megan marries a guy in a bowling league and never goes to college. Let's explore this notion more carefully by going back to the night of the prom.

Megan goes to bed. Her sleep is filled with dreams that interpret their own disturbance, leaving her with nothing to think about when she wakes up. She feels restless for most of the morning, disappointed that the magical feeling that came out of nowhere the night before hasn't already made a profound difference in how she sees the world. But then she remembers a point she made in a fight with a friend a week before, that sudden transformations take place only in Hollywood movies, which means that what she felt the previous night should only be seen as a point of departure, that it's *her* job to improve her life by taking intelligent actions. So she goes to the mall and buys a copy of *Das Kapital*, having heard so much about it from her very cool economics teacher. But aside from a few compelling phrases, she finds the first few pages dull or incomprehensible. She feels so stupid that after graduating she decides not to go to college, even though she's got good grades. She gets a job in the cocktail lounge of the neighborhood bowling alley, a place where the fifties never died, where the men slick back their hair and wear cigarette packs in rolled-up sleeves.

One night a very nice man with glasses, curly hair, and no rolled up sleeves comes in from the street to get change for a twenty. He shyly catches her eye and they talk. He comes in again the next week and they talk. He comes in again the next week and they talk and he asks her out on a date. They go to a small café on a cliff by the sea, where the men are all unshaven, look brilliantly confused and talk about jazz and quantum physics, while the women wear sweatshirts, look brilliantly confused, and talk about jazz and gender. She likes it because it reminds her of her twelfth-grade economics class. After she's been there several times with the very nice man, she tells him that she wants to quit her job and move in with him. He tells her that he doesn't have a job, has no plans to get one any time soon, and just wants to collect unemployment, listen to jazz, and read about physics. If he has to support someone else, he'll have to get a job, and when she offers to be the primary breadwinner, supporting him by continuing to work as a cocktail waitress, he refuses because he's a very nice man and doesn't want to take advantage of anyone.

She's crushed. She doesn't believe his excuse. She thinks that if she were better looking, he wouldn't have hesitated. Severe feelings of inferiority come up, reminding her of the night when everyone else was at the prom. She tells herself she's in love with the very nice man, that she wants to stay with him no matter what. But she thinks that he's probably just being nice while he slowly tries to get rid of her, and that if she keeps trying to see him, he'll have to be blunt. She can't bear the thought of what he might say.

The next time he calls, she wants to say she's got a cold and can't go out. But she's too afraid of losing him, so she says that she's eager to see him, that she'll meet him at the café in half an hour. Megan starts getting ready but something tells her not to. She stops and sits in a chair by the only window in her small apartment, gazing out over the rooftops toward the silhouettes of factory smokestacks in a glorious late spring sunset. Between her passion for the very nice man, her assumption that he's looking for a painless way to get rid of her, her aversion to the sparse furnishings of her cramped apartment, and her frustration at being too distracted to fully enjoy the sunset, a difficult feeling emerges, as if the words that normally tell her what she's feeling were telling her that she's feeling something else, making her seem to be living on the street in a cardboard box. She feels her breath getting shorter, the window seems to be moving away, and the floor is like a page in someone's notebook. She knows that the simplest thing to do would be to tell the very nice man to go fuck himself, but the simplest thing isn't always the best, despite the many religious teachings that urge you to strip the complexity from your mind and locate the simple truth that's always there if you can just be honest with yourself. Megan doesn't like religious teachings, and she's never been good at telling herself the truth. Indeed, the truth looks like the alarm clock on the windowsill beside her bed, making her seem to be the protagonist in a convoluted narrative whose meaning cracks like an egg in the reader's hands.

We've come to the crucial point. According to the many-worlds approach to quantum physics, Megan meets the very nice man at the cafe and they keep seeing each other, while at the same time she calls him back and tells him to go fuck himself. The first possibility might lead us back to the neo-Marxist outcome, and there's no need to tell the same story twice. So it makes sense at this point to move in the other direction.

Megan picks up the phone and tells the very nice man to go fuck himself. Within a year she's married to a man with slicked-back hair and a cigarette pack rolled up in his sleeve. He turns out to be a reliable husband and father to their children, but he's at the bowling alley three nights a week, and the other nights he falls asleep on the couch with the TV on. It's not a great life, but the man does offer Megan some very nice things. He's got a big dick, a steady job, and tells her she's beautiful at least three times a week. She starts to believe she's better looking than she thought she was, and soon she's no longer dominated by the feeling that everyone is disappointed when they look at her. Her improved self-image allows her to more fully enjoy the parties he takes her to. It's true that they don't have much in common, very few shared conversational interests, but they both like talking about the weather at length, and this fills gaps that might otherwise be disturbing.

But one night she feels anxious and confused after reading a magazine article about women who ruin their lives by getting married and having kids too soon, trapping themselves in limited situations. She looks at her husband snoring on the couch. She looks at her two little boys, arguing so fiercely over a game of Chutes & Ladders that they don't even know she's in the room. She does something she's never done before. Without a word, Megan leaves the house and takes a walk.

She's nervous at first, surprised by what she's doing. But soon she begins to enjoy the feeling of simply walking, the sound her footsteps make on the sidewalk, the stiff breeze on the cobbled street, the silhouettes of gabled housetops, the moonlit clouds reflected in top-floor windows. She stops to sit on a bench. Again we're at a crucial point, face to face with the bifurcating options predicted by the many-worlds theory. In one of these options, the moon goes behind a cloud and the street disappears, leaving Megan to contemplate the absence of the world, the absence even of absence, a condition she finds unnerving at first, but slowly it begins to sound like music, a vast orchestration of nothingness, moving her so profoundly that she decides to become someone else.

She gets a room for the night in a small hotel, finds herself an apartment the following day, a cozy waterfront place where she develops her own meditation technique, learning how to read the light and shade on her broad oak floorboards. She becomes so immersed in what she's doing that she never thinks of going home, and as she refines her meditation process, she finds herself moving deeper and deeper into a deepening silence, which takes the visual form of a dim corridor, two half-open doors on either side, and from each room she can almost hear a different section of a jazz composition, four sections performed at once or performed in sequence, depending on how she listens, her position in relation to the corridor, which vanishes like smoke in sudden wind if she looks too closely, a disappearance that frustrates her at first, but soon she learns to enjoy what isn't quite there, the possibility of music, the subtle ecstasy of something that hasn't happened yet, and doesn't need to.

In a second option, the moon goes behind a cloud and everything stays right where it is, though of course the street is darker, making her want the comforts of her living room, the bickering of her little boys, the snoring of her husband in front of a televised football game. She goes home convinced that she's discovered a new kind of happiness, the pleasure of simply walking, not knowing where she's going, an expansive feeling that has the potential to balance the limitations of her domestic life. Suddenly the notion of getting married too soon doesn't seem so menacing. After all, she tells herself, many women have it worse than she does, and besides, she knows that if she reads the right magazines, she can find articles claiming that to have a good marriage, both partners need to appreciate what they have.

Of course, it's hard to see the virtues of your situation when you're forced to confront it day after day, and at least three times a week she feels like moving to the moon. But now she's found a way to keep things fresh. Whenever she feels trapped, she goes out for long walks, sometimes for hours and hours, sometimes all night long. She's pleasantly amazed that her husband and kids don't object, and this leads her to love them even more, no matter how dull they often are. She tells herself she's found what all the magazine articles told her to find, a way to appreciate what she has, and soon she's become an expert on maintaining a positive attitude, each day making a brand-new list of things to be grateful for, keeping a journal of what she sees when she wanders through the city.

But soon she begins to notice how words refuse to merely describe, how she always ends up with something she didn't plan to write. At first she takes this to be a sign of incompetence, assuming that if she were in command of the process, the pages of her journal would verbally replicate her surroundings. If she wanted to write about sunlight flashing on the chrome of a passing school bus, she wouldn't end up writing about an alien spacecraft landing by mistake in an urban park. If she wanted to write about a clown disguised as a college art instructor, she wouldn't end up writing about a book of prehistoric symbols. If she wanted to write about radios filling public space with big-hit noise pollution, she wouldn't end up writing about a mystic making a massive rock appear on a high school basketball court. If she wanted to write about a woman having fun with *Moby-Dick*, blessing its author and throwing the book off the edge of a cliff by the sea, she wouldn't end up writing about lovers defying the gods by having too much fun in bed. If she wanted to write about a man with a map in his pocket getting lost in a maze of urban streets, she wouldn't end up writing about two middle-aged men in Pink Floyd sweatshirts reading the same rare book in a loud café, with M. C. Escher posters on the walls. If she wanted her words to behave, they would behave. But as things currently stand, her words don't want to be told what to say. Her frustration builds over the next few months, until she decides that she'll either have to stop writing altogether, or accept that the words are in command, that they can't or won't reproduce the world, that the world is nothing more than a point of verbal departure.

The more she lets her language find its own way, the more her life begins to feel like someone else's life, as if she were someone someone else was writing about in a story, and her goal was to find out who that writer was. Over time, this preoccupation destroys her life at home. When she tries to explain why she doesn't feel like herself any longer, why she feels that there's always someone else deciding what she does, someone who exists in another dimension, someone whose face might suddenly replace her face in a mirror, her husband assumes that either she's crazy or she's having an affair, and the courts agree that she's not a fit mother anymore, awarding him custody of their kids when he gets a divorce. Soon she's begging for change on the streets, living in a cardboard box in a city park, claiming that she's writing on pages of water, that the words themselves are telling her what to write, that the journal she's keeping is a UFO, an unidentified fictive object that comes from another planet, a place whose inhabitants travel through time and space in the form of language, living in the words and thoughts of the populations they encounter.

At this point bifurcation again occurs. In option number one, Megan's husband finds her starving on the streets and has a change of heart, taking her back into his home and finding her the psychiatric help she badly needs. For almost a year, she spends most of her time in bed, mentally wandering like someone following dubious maps through towering mountains, but at the same time she's watching the world in the window, slowly letting time and space replace the chaos of words in her head.

In option number two, her husband plays no part. Megan continues to live in a cardboard box, or rather, she lives the last few days of her life in the journal she's been keeping, learning to surrender, giving language full control, watching as the personality she's been haunted by starts to reveal himself on the page, telling a story that challenges readers to think about their social interactions. Megan sees a younger version of herself in one of the characters, a woman so unpopular that no one wants to take her to the prom. Though her vision is starting to fade and the page appears to be slowly moving away, Megan likes the narrator's way of questioning things that are normally taken for granted. She's eager to see what happens at the end, to see if he maintains his skeptical view of dates and parties. But the page keeps moving farther away, her breath is getting shorter, and Megan dies at precisely the point that her name first appears in the story.

ECSTATIC ELLIPSIS

During the early seventies, it was common to hear people claim to be high on life. They generally made this pious declaration after giving up drugs and cutting their hair, turning their backs on the revolution to find full-time jobs, get married and raise families, becoming respectable members of society.

Cora James and her boyfriend Barry never said they were high on life. They always made sure they were high on drugs, especially psychedelics. Yes, they found respectable jobs after graduating from college—both worked as community college reference librarians. But they carefully avoided becoming adults. In the twenty-five years that they lived with each other, they never had a TV set, never read

Time or *Newsweek*, never hired an accountant, never owned a house, never bothered with party politics, never bought new cars, never got legally married, never stopped making love, never had kids. They lived as if time and space were cartoon characters.

But one day Barry took too much acid and thought he saw big presidential faces carved into the cliffs visible in the distance from their top-floor apartment. Suddenly the thought of tripping at Mount Rushmore became irresistible. A few weeks later, once the spring semester was over, Barry and Cora were traveling east from the Oregon coast, having scored what one of their friends called the best Orange Sunshine south of the North Pole.

They passed through magnificent places on their way to see the presidents, mountains and mesas and rivers and valleys that normally would have been ideal sites for psychedelic sightseeing. But if they'd been tripping the whole time, they might have been burned-out by the time they got to the Black Hills. They took their tabs as soon as they got to the Mount Rushmore information center, then spent the rest of the day laughing as tourists in patriotic t-shirts desperately photographed everything in sight. They stayed up all night watching the big stone presidents basking in a hundred spotlights, changing into each other, a blue Jefferson becoming a red Lincoln, a green Washington becoming a blue Lincoln, a green Roosevelt becoming a yellow Jefferson, a red Washington becoming a blue Roosevelt.

When the lights were finally turned off, Cora thought it might be fun to sit on Washington's face, and before too long they were perched on his majestic forehead, watching the pre-dawn light gathering behind the mountains. The

first beams of sunlight burst over the Black Hills like spray
from huge waves breaking on rocks, congealing into huge
amoebas, elongating themselves to become snakes rising
out of Medusa's head, snapping free to become a thousand
iridescent birds of prey, all converging on Barry and driving
him off the edge of Washington's head. The prismatic folds
of the air parted in front of him and closed in back of him, a
disappearance so mesmerizing that Cora didn't understand
for several hours that Barry was dead two hundred feet
below.

Cora's life went downhill after that. Drugs were no fun
without Barry, and making new friends was difficult. Most of
the middle-aged people she met were busy raising children,
and most of the younger people wanted younger people as
friends. So she put her social life on hold and started pursuing
a life-long dream, taking painting classes at the college where
she worked. Her first completed pictures impressed her professor, who told her she had talent as a landscape painter. But
Cora didn't call what she was doing landscape painting. She
thought of visual art in terms of sound. She heard melodies
in her head and made them pines bending in cold wind on a
cloudy afternoon, or a lake reflecting mountains, or a ghost
town filled with tumbleweed in moonlight, and when the
picture was done she knew it was really spatialized music,
though no one else saw anything more than a vividly painted
place. Were Cora's paintings musical notation in disguise?
Should avant-garde musicians have been inspired to learn
how to play Cora's landscapes?

She thought of these possibilities, but the problem was
painfully clear. Her paintings obscured the music, transforming it into something she felt no connection to. Even if others

got visual pleasure from her work, she knew they weren't really sharing what she felt when she made the paintings. No matter how many art classes she took over the next three years at different community colleges, no matter how many supportive responses she got from her teachers, she always felt that her pictures were imprecise translations.

Her final teacher, who made extra money as a birthday clown when he wasn't in the classroom, told her that the music of inspiration was irrelevant, nothing more than a point of departure. The only thing that mattered was what ended up on the canvas. She came to his office to discuss this comment further.

He said: When I'm in the painting mood, my head fills with words, whispered instructions, and often the voices contradict each other. When they first started talking to me, back in my early twenties, I was confused. But then I realized that the painting was meant to come from the contradiction, the space the conflicting voices couldn't quite occupy.

Through the window behind his head, Cora could see a sky of nimbus clouds, flags on a cluster of carnival tents with a Ferris wheel in the background, a billboard ad with lumberjacks and perky blondes in a rustic bar, a huge dead maple tree beside an abandoned railroad station.

Cora said: The space the conflicting voices couldn't quite occupy? That's an interesting way to put it. But I'm not sure what you mean. Are you talking about the space between the different *meanings* of what your voices tell you, or the space between the different *mental sounds* the two voices make?

He paused and stared at the empty goldfish bowl on his desk. Then he said: If one voice claims that A is B and another one claims that A is F, then the painting has to be C+D+E, or D+E+C, or E+D+C, or C+E+D, or D+C+E, or E+C+D.

Cora could hear faint laughter in her head. She said: Is this some kind of a joke?

The teacher said: I never joke unless I'm dressed as a clown. Nothing is more serious than a clown out of uniform.

Cora said: But doesn't it bother you that the voices in your head never have a chance to express themselves directly?

The teacher said: The voices in my head belong in my head, just like a fish in a goldfish bowl belongs in the goldfish bowl. If you take the fish out of the bowl, you'll have a dead fish. The music in your head belongs in your head. Painting is something you do with your hands and a paintbrush.

Cora wanted to think that her teacher was making good sense. But something about the thought of him dressed as a clown made anything but technical instruction sound absurd. Besides, Cora loved what she heard in her head. She wanted to paint its color and shape. She didn't want to think of it as a dead fish. The comparison made her angry. So the next time she came to class she brought a painting of a dead goldfish, dry and hard beside a goldfish bowl on a coffee table. When her teacher said it was her best painting of the semester, Cora walked out of the classroom and never came back.

She decided there was no point in taking more classes, but without the classroom setting she couldn't get herself to keep painting. Instead, she started drinking, at first by herself with her favorite sixties rock songs blasting in her living room, then in bars where she spent long nights with lonely middle-aged men. One man in particular caught her attention. The more scotch he drank the smarter he became, discoursing brilliantly on the history of stupidity in America, trashing especially the founding fathers, reserving special scorn for Hamilton and Jefferson, claiming that the only one who would have been fun to talk to was Ben "Fart Proudly" Franklin.

After many nights of bitter laughter, they agreed to meet for lunch, the first time they'd ever seen each other in sober sunlight. Without scotch, the man was obsessed with the details of Custer's Last Stand, refusing to talk about anything else, presenting elaborate arguments that supposedly proved that Custer survived the Little Bighorn and was later sighted many times in Memphis and New Orleans, where he opened brothels and bars, got involved with local politics, and joined the Ku Klux Klan. Cora told herself not to get annoyed, to nod and smile, and never to meet the man sober again. In fact, she refused to meet anyone outside the bar again.

Before too long, she knew she was becoming an alcoholic, even though she hated being drunk. She and Barry had always agreed that drinking was inferior to drugging as a way to get high, that grass and hash and especially LSD were subversive substances, while excessive drinking was merely a sign of conformity or failure. But when she couldn't seem to stop, she joined Alcoholics Anonymous, where she was quickly told that she needed the help of a higher power. She'd never believed in God, so she did the next best thing, getting a sponsor who thought of himself as a substitute for God. He insisted that their relationship would never end up in the bedroom, that the AA traditions clearly stated that newcomers should avoid romantic relationships for at least nine months.

But nine weeks later they were making love, and nine weeks after that they were living together, and nine weeks after that she was already bored. The sex was great but the man had no sense of humor, and claimed that he always told the truth no matter how painful it was. Instinctively, Cora hated people who never laughed and never lied. The fun she had in bed was enough to keep her from looking for somebody else, but to get away from the pious platitudes he was fond of reciting, she soon decided she had to find a better higher power.

Since God was out of the question, she tried meditation classes. The difference was clear at once. While God and the man she'd substituted for God were authority figures, meditation focused on the rhythm of her breathing. The only authority figure was her body. This came with its own set of challenges, difficult memories trapped in zones of neuro-muscular tension. But it wasn't the same as being in church, or being with someone who thought he knew what everyone ought to be doing.

Her lover became enraged when she started avoiding AA meetings, relying on meditation to keep herself sober. They began fighting on a regular basis, but their conflict pattern soon became so predictable that neither really heard what the other was saying.

He would say: I know you've got a crush on that self-righteous creep you meditate with. If I ever find out that you've been in bed with him, he'll be swallowing his teeth and you'll be living in the street.

Instead of his words, she would hear a fly buzzing in an old hotel room, a fool ecstatically singing his way through remote mountain valleys, eggs and bacon popping and snapping on a skillet, an airplane taking off on a foggy runway.

She would look out the window and see the sky becoming a huge umbrella, or a dirty glass of water, or a blackboard with a paragraph getting erased, and she would try to read the words before they disappeared, or try to see whose eager hand was making the blackboard blank. Then she would look her lover in the eye and say: You keep telling me that there's only one fucking way to stay sober: *your* way. I can't stand it any longer! I get more out of listening to the sound of my own goddamn breathing than I get from listening to the self-serving advice you can't seem to stop dishing out.

Instead of her words, he would hear frogs croaking in a pond at four in the morning, a balloon getting popped in a closet, a muzak version of a jazz classic in a supermarket, polite applause in response to the sound of an arrow splitting an apple.

She moved out as soon as she could, having found what seemed like a gift from God: an inexpensive top-floor apartment overlooking a forest, a quiet place with a partial view of the ocean in the distance. It was a great setting for meditation, and she told herself that silence and not painting was the best medium for the shapes of sound in her head. But she knew it was wrong to trust a gift from God. A month after moving in, she lost her job to budget cutbacks, and three months later she lost her home when the landlord sold the building. There was nothing to do but move in with her born-again Christian brother and his family, an arrangement which went from oppressive to impossible when a doctor told her she had only one year to live.

Her brother thought he knew just what to do, asking ministers from his church to make a house call. After listening gravely to the story of her life, they decided that her disease was a divine punishment for doing so much LSD and living in sin for twenty-five years. They told her she might be saved if she could just get down on her knees and ask the Lord to come into her life. She listened politely, nodding and smiling. Then she said she had a headache and went upstairs to bed. Falling asleep was like dropping into the open jaws of a whale, or into a nightmare bowling alley, where she worked as a cocktail waitress forcing herself to smile through noise and cigarette smoke at aggressively stupid men.

But one of the men looked familiar, spoke with Barry's voice, seemed to be right beside her in bed, holding her and laughing, talking about their favorite crackpot scientific theories. Suddenly something jerked her awake, and she was telling herself that even if quantum scientists, at some point in the distant future, devised a way of traveling into the prehistoric past, people who made the journey would quickly be sacrificed, offered up to the gods of time and space, burned or hacked apart on sacred altars, according to a cosmic law stipulating that if the past was altered even slightly, the present would collapse, shattered by reverberations caused by the mere presence of modern behavior in ancient times. With Barry, such ideas would have been funny, but by herself in a house of born-again Christians, she felt menaced, afraid to go back to sleep, so she searched her bedroom for something to read. She found an old but unused notebook on a shelf in an empty closet. Since the empty pages felt like invitations, she began writing, imagining that words had magic powers, allowing her to exist in many places at once, allowing her to see that each place was many different places, as if each word were a liquid map, an aquarium filled with the graceful colors and motions of tropical fish. At three in the morning she tiptoed out the back door and never came back.

Now she's by herself in a slowly collapsing Victorian mansion, an elaborate collection of cupolas and gables propped on a seaside cliff. It's a place everyone has somehow forgotten about, realtors included, so that no one plans to buy, rent, or tear it down. She's living on nothing more than a mattress and blanket she found in a thrift shop, falling asleep each night on a huge wrap-around porch, entranced by the sound of waves on rocks and the damp wind in the trees. She's mastering the art of getting by on almost nothing, slowly using up the two thousand dollars left in her savings account, surviving on one small meal a day. The more accustomed she gets to modest amounts of carefully chosen food, the more it seems to give her what she needs and even what she wants. She goes without electricity, gets water from a creek behind her house, and pees and shits in the woods. There's nothing within five miles but forest and ocean, with one dirt road that no one ever uses. She carefully limits herself to superficial contact with the town the dirt road leads to, walking there for meager supplies once every two weeks, speaking only to get what she needs. The townspeople think she's crazy, and at times she thinks so too, but it slowly becomes clear to her that she's free in a way she never expected, even as she struggles with a terminal disease, the pain that tells her time is running out.

At first the stormy climate is her primary source of pleasure. Four nights out of five the wind is so strong that her blanket is barely enough, and the feeling of almost being hopelessly cold—almost but not quite—is so delicious that she never thinks of going inside. Soon she begins equating it with another delicious feeling, the release from conversations of any length and complexity, the freedom from needing to make a verbal account of herself, transferring mental energy from the sphere of interaction to the sphere of perception, allowing her to observe herself in the increasingly transparent mirror held up by the non-human universe, instead of in the aggressive mirror of human complexity and distortion, a transformation that might be compared to shadows thrown from a sluggish overhead fan, endlessly gliding over a carved oak desk, where a pensive man with an old fedora sits in a small stone room, squinting into the glare outside, miles on miles of desert sand and homicidal sunlight, knowing that as long as he stays in the shade he'll survive the brutal heat, and reports come in by phone, vital information, making him nod and smile, but he's anxious about one crucial unreturned phone call, the climax of a plan to seize the wealth of the ruling class worldwide, evenly redistributing their criminal accumulations, and he blows tense air out of his mouth, tries to relax in the turning shadows, which make the map of the world on the wall seem graceful as an aquarium, continents and oceans blending with words to become an ecstatic design, a lovely feeling he's had in the past but can't quite access now, trapped in the fear that everything he's been working toward for the past five years—all his elaborate networking from a small stone house in the middle of nowhere—has come to nothing, anxiety that brings him to

the edge of madness as the minutes pass and the light outside his cool dark square gets hotter, and the silence made
by miles and miles of shifting sand gets hotter, reaching the
point where it has to become something else, giving way to
an empty city street at three in the morning, silence broken
only by the sound of an old man's footsteps, darkness flat
as a blackboard framing a tiny square of light, a dormer
window five blocks away, a room where a young man studies
a battered book, a series of woodcuts, abstract images that
have nothing to do with any known system of knowledge,
but seem to have been composed for a definite purpose, perhaps by a community of magicians who lived in stone huts in
the mountains west of the Caspian Sea four thousand years
ago, people who lived only to generate an evolving pattern
of ecstatic designs, a collection of sacred pages passed on
in secret for almost forty centuries, reproduced as woodcuts
in the early Middle Ages, randomly dispersed throughout
the Middle East and southern Europe, gathered and bound
in a single volume somewhere in Armenia during the Re-
naissance, passing through the hands of many collectors all
over the world, then finally discarded, classified as a fraud,
gathering dust for more than two hundred years, until an
unemployed mathematician came across it in a second-hand
bookstore in lower Manhattan, and he's been lost in its pages
ever since, caught in a migrating spell of images and phrases
that seem to lead nowhere, like a dictionary of words that
don't exist yet, all defined by words that don't exist yet, like
an eye the size of an ocean liner closing in a midnight sky, a
mile and a half above the tallest iceberg in the Bering Sea,
or like the prospect of walking for days toward what seems
to be a towering metropolis, only to find after a brutal trek

that the city is no larger than it looked at first, that its tallest buildings are perhaps ten inches high, that it takes up less than five square feet, and that the population has no time for baffled, obnoxious giants, or like a sleepwalker walking downstairs while dreaming of walking upstairs, mesmerized by the sound of his feet on the stairs, a turning marble staircase in the dark of intergalactic space, glowing and steadily growing until it becomes a new constellation, or like a UFO visitation erasing itself in the minds of observers, replacing the experience with the memory of a sci-fi flick, a flying-saucer movie millions of people are convinced they've seen, but it's so bad no one ever thinks of watching it again, or like a chimpanzee that learns to talk after less than a year of instruction, but carefully pretends that he understands nothing, screeching and scratching his head, knowing that he's better off not speaking, and that he has nothing to say, or nothing that he *wants* to say in the language he's been learning, or like the surgical process of opening the body of an extremely sad person and finding a smaller ecstatic version of the same person inside, then cutting open that ecstatic body and finding a map of the universe inside, a map that no one can read without going mad, or like a microscopic tenor saxophone charming an amoeba, or like an absurd list of images that refuse to play a supporting role, abducting the narrative they appear to be embellishing, triggering only dissolving associations that have nothing to do with the unemployed mathematician's personal past, but otherwise behave like distant memories, making his past appear to be much larger than it was, larger than anyone's past could possibly be, in the same way that a wilderness is always much larger than the dirt road passing through it, leaving him on the edge of a trance, gazing beyond the battered book of images on his desk, haunted by the distinct impression of having walked all night through an unfamiliar city, accompanied only by the sound of his own footsteps in a maze of empty streets, pausing at three in the morning to stare at a square of light in the distance, a dormer window becoming a door of desert light and silence, unbearable heat and sand for hundreds of miles in every direction, a small stone room, a carved oak desk and a man with an old fedora, staring into the tension of shadows thrown from an overhead fan, but then the phone call comes and the news is good, and after pausing to confirm the information, jotting down a few numbers in his notebook, he leans back in his chair and laughs with every cell in his body, laughter so intense that the rest of the world seems unimportant, making the house and the desert sand and the sky look flat and small and framed, nothing more than a painting on a wall in someone's kitchen, where people are eating with such pleasure that the food on the table just barely avoids becoming a meal of words on a page, a situation that might be compared to what happens when Cora James decides that she doesn't want to be bothered with conventional responsibilities any longer, and begins to look at herself in the unassuming mirror held up by the non-human universe, instead of in the intrusive mirror of human complexity and distortion.

Cora takes in three stray dogs and develops a playful, tender relationship with each one, a telepathic intimacy that goes beyond the cumbersome feelings verbal language confines most people to. This intimacy undermines the syntactic architecture she's learned to equate with subjective experience, so thoroughly transforming her perceptions that she begins to hear separations, subtle distinctions between the sound of one wave and the next, between each leaf and every other leaf in the strong and steady wind, between each raindrop tapping on each leaf and on the roof of the porch, and she carefully studies the many ways that all the different sounds combine to make one general sound, elaborately varied patterns of divergence and convergence that she learns to call music, blending with the musical shapes that hover just behind her eyes, until finally the distinction between music and everything that's not music disintegrates, as if the mansion were nothing more than the sound of rain and wind and waves and maybe just words on a page, and maybe not even words, not even a page or a face bending over the page, not even a face in the dark, not even the dark, just fading footsteps, and death brings no pain at all—no regret or fear of the unknown—only the ecstasy of dissolving into a musical world she's learned to perceive so carefully that she finally can't say she's even listening to it, since listening implies that she's somehow distinct from what she's listening to. In short, what could only be a question mark for anyone else becomes in her final glimpse of time and space an ecstatic ellipsis.

Within a few months, realtors discover the house and put it on the market. A group of five avant-garde composers purchase the place at a give-away price. They begin to fix it up and turn it into a center for progressive music, a project they've been planning for years, providing a space for themselves and their colleagues to write music and give performances. Three dogs greet them eagerly when they arrive. Throughout the first month, while the composers work to get the place in shape, the dogs entice them into playful games, sitting at their feet and licking their faces, adding so much joy to the place that the men decide to adopt them.

One of the first musicians in residence at the center is Moira Jones, a well-known composer struggling to complete what she knows might become the greatest piece of her life. For the past three years, she hasn't been able to figure out the ending, even though she thinks about it all the time, even though she's known throughout the music world as a master of endings. Now she's at the center on a fellowship, hoping that a few months of oceanic silence will coax the music out of its hiding place. Moira's compositions are based on visual constructions, rapidly changing pictures that develop in her mind, shapes that dissolve into sounds and patterns of sound. The current piece begins with an oval mirror, which then becomes a wineglass, a corncob pipe, a kettledrum, a megaphone, a pyramid, a waterfall, a fishbowl. But she can't get past the fishbowl, which sits on a windowsill and looks like it hasn't been used in twenty-five years, making her feel like someone who can't wake up, or someone in a cinematic freeze-frame.

She's always hated asking for help or advice, but she's feeling desperate, and several times she discusses her problem with the center's directors, three of whom are trained as music therapists. They all tell her the same thing—to relax, make herself laugh, let the problem solve itself. The suggestion sounds good at first, but later annoys her, especially after she's heard it several times and can't figure out how to put it into practice. It's not that she was expecting technical advice—and in any case she wouldn't have let anyone tell her how to revise her music—but she does want something more specific than what she's been told. When she visits the composers again, one of them tells her to do some dope, but grass and hash have always made her paranoid, and her older brother flipped out on LSD. Another one tries to teach her how to meditate, but her body isn't flexible enough to sit in the lotus position, and she's too worked up to sit still for even a minute. Another one tells her to rent comedies from the video store in town. But scripted humor never makes her laugh. It makes her mad.

Her ex was a stand-up comedian. She married him because they thought she was pregnant, before she knew him well enough to know how self-absorbed he was, how he always needed approval and applause, how he thought he was the only funny person in the world. The mere thought of him gets her angry, his offensive routines about hippies and radicals, all of whom were hypocrites, according to the supposedly funny stories he told on stage. The story she hated most was based on people who said they were high on life, a skit that made it seem that hippies who stopped doing drugs were closet conservatives, and hippies who never stopped doing drugs were out-of-the-closet morons. Moira decided that behind his jokes he was little more than a right-wing pig.

Her own career was developing quite nicely. But the more recognition she got, the more he tried to undermine her confidence, claiming that her music wasn't playful enough, that it was too stiff and pompous to be convincing. Whenever he said this, her unexpressed anger took her back twelve thousand years, back to the edge of a Stone Age village, and she found herself on a trail in a dense forest, drawn by the smell of an approaching thunderstorm, finally reaching a sacrificial altar in a clearing, where three men gripping sharp stone objects, knives apparently, came at her with absurdly somber expressions that filled her with laughter. But her therapist insisted that laughter was an evasive way of dealing with anger, that she was better off exploding than hiding what she felt.

The crisis finally came in their third year of marriage, when one of Moira's compositions got a rave review in *The New York Times*. He said the reviewer was clearly a mental midget. A fight began which climaxed when she smashed an oval mirror they'd inherited from his mother, shouting that he never should have been with her in the first place, since he knew what her music was like before they met. He met her violence with a calculated smile that haunted her for years to come, quietly declaring that ever since the doctor told her she wasn't really pregnant, her music had been a lifeless imitation of itself. Within a year, she was single, and she hasn't let anyone touch her since. But now she's been told again that she's too serious, that she needs to relax. Rage keeps her up all night. The word *serious* bangs at her window like a bare branch in gusting wind.

At three in the morning she finally gives up and turns on the light in her bedroom. Looking for something to read, she finds an old notebook in her closet. Every page contains just one paragraph, the same paragraph, eight sentences that apparently have nothing to do with each other, and on each page the passage has been crossed out. There's nothing else in the book, no other writing of any kind. And the handwriting is identical throughout—exactly the same words appear on each line, and every letter is formed in the same way every time it's used. Even the lines that cross out the writing are the same on each page, neat and firm, leaving no doubt that the

passage was a mistake. She keeps turning the pages, expecting some kind of difference, looking closely, hoping to find
even inconspicuous changes, maybe a comma that doesn't
look the same as the other commas, maybe a period made a
tiny bit larger than the rest. But everything is always exactly
the same, and she decides that since the writing itself never
changes, she needs to focus on herself, on what she thinks,
feels, and imagines while she reads, on how her perceptions
change from page to page.

She returns to the start and begins again with different
expectations, reading as if the book were a series of canceled
incantations. She tries to bring the magic back by slowly reciting the words, immersing herself in her voice: "I sit in an
abandoned high school classroom watching a sunrise. I sit in
an airport lounge and stare at a huge clock stopped at half
past five. I sit in a health-food restaurant facing the ruins of
a cathedral. I sit on the bank of a river surging with ice and
afternoon sunlight. I sit on the steps of an old screen porch
as a lightning storm approaches. I sit on a swaying footbridge
watching coyotes hunt in the canyon below. I sit at the foot of
a dead tree on a ridge above an amusement park. I sit in fog
on a gabled housetop overlooking a junkyard."

Something strange takes place. Though the words on
the page remain the same, by the end of the book the words
coming out of her mouth have changed completely, making
her the main character in the narrative they're composing:
"At three in the morning she finally gives up and turns on
the light in her bedroom. Looking for something to read,
she finds an old notebook in her closet. Every page contains
just one paragraph, the same paragraph, eight sentences that
apparently have nothing to do with each other, and on each

page the passage has been crossed out. There's nothing else in the book, no other writing of any kind. And the handwriting is identical throughout—exactly the same words appear on each line, and every letter is formed in the same way every time it's used. Even the lines that cross out the writing are the same on each page, neat and firm, leaving no doubt that the passage was a mistake."

She stops her voice and takes a closer look at the canceled passage. Each sentence on its own looks like the start of something else, a narrative involving people, places, and events. But page after page, the sentences introduce nothing. Instead they leave her in many places at once, mesmerized by a constellation of undefined possibilities, multiple futures that never take place, distances that never come any closer. The feeling was disconcerting at first, but now she looks at the page with different expectations, watching the sentences changing into each other, watching the syllables turn and glide and swim in a liquid medium, as if she were slowly becoming an aquarium filled with tropical fish, a graceful pattern of colors and motions, a moment changing only to resemble itself, reassemble itself, a quiet feeling of almost absolute safety.

She thinks of Coltrane's classic, *A Love Supreme*, the turbulent feeling of safety it's always given her. It's been her favorite piece of music for twenty-five years, ever since her father asked to hear it on his deathbed. But somehow the final section eludes her now. The somber saxophone melody barely surviving the furious drumming—Moira knows each note by heart. Yet now the sound is somewhere else, and she feels like an actress who can't hear the soundtrack of the film she's got the lead role in.

Instead she hears an argument from her past, musicians in a bar in Lower Manhattan, laughing when she said that *A Love Supreme* was her favorite album. She can still hear the booming voice of a bearded man with a baseball hat: Coltrane is bullshit. The only Coltrane I can listen to at all is the stuff he did at the end of his life. If you like jazz, forget about Coltrane and try some Ornette Coleman.

She didn't like people trashing music she liked, and she'd always felt that Coleman's music was more fun to talk about than to listen to. But she held her annoyance in check and said: I *did* like an album he did with Don Cherry, Billy Higgins, Freddie Hubbard, and Charlie Haden, with two quartets playing different things at the same time.

He said: Right, that's called *Free Jazz*. Now *there* you've got something worth listening to. But no one's ever heard of Ornette Coleman because they're too busy talking about Coltrane all the time—or Miles Davis. But Coltrane never would've gotten past *My Favorite Things* if he hadn't heard Coleman's quartet at the Five Spot back in 1960. Coltrane's whole avant-garde phase was triggered by Ornette Coleman. The best thing you can say about Coltrane was that his ego didn't get in the way. He admitted that Ornette was making the music of the future, and even asked him for lessons. Ever heard this story? They met at Coleman's apartment several times, and Ornette apparently taught him a few things, I'm not sure what. A few months later, when Coltrane made some money from one of his albums, he sent Ornette a long thank-you letter, along with thirty dollars for every lesson. And Ornette was surprised because their meetings had been so informal, not like lessons at all, though I'm guessing if they were talking about music things got pretty intense.

It's been a long time since Moira cared if *Free Jazz* was more avant-garde than *A Love Supreme*. But she's still moved by the thought of Coltrane admitting that Coleman had something to teach him, putting his desire to learn above anything else. In her own career, she hasn't done the same. Instead, she's been driven by a fierce desire to be seen as a major composer, to get as many reviews and grants and gigs as possible. She's always regarded her colleagues as competitors, not as people struggling with more or less the same aesthetic problems, people who might offer something she can learn from or be inspired by. But Coltrane was always eager to learn from anyone.

She looks back at the notebook, the cancelled incantation. Something tells her to read the pages again, and again by the end of the book the words coming out of her mouth have become something else. But this time she's convinced that they're describing another person: "Finally the distinction between music and everything that's not music disintegrates, as if the mansion were nothing more than the sound of rain and wind and waves and maybe just words on a page, and maybe not even words, not even a page or a face bending over the page, not even a face in the dark, not even the dark, just fading footsteps, and death brings no pain at all—no regret or fear of the unknown—only the ecstasy of dissolving into a musical world she's learned to perceive so carefully that she finally can't say she's even listening to it, since listening implies that she's somehow distinct from what she's listening to. In short, what could only be a question mark for anyone else becomes in her final glimpse of time and space an ecstatic ellipsis."

She looks outside. The waves aren't quite as dark as

they were before, which means that the sun is probably starting to rise on the other side of the house. She goes downstairs
and stands on the porch, then walks to the edge of the cliff,
gazing out at the ridge of mist where the ocean meets the
sky. The dogs burst out of the darkness, chasing each other
across the lawn. One of them turns to pursue a gull, which
waits until it's just about to get caught before flying away.
Another sits and chews a bone, thinking with his teeth. The
third one sits at her feet and licks her hand, looks eagerly into
the depth of her eyes. Her body feels like a huge aquarium
filled with tropical fish. Now she knows exactly what to do
with her composition.

She changes it so radically that it doesn't need an ending. It makes the very notion of an ending obsolete.

COLLAPSING INTO A STORY

I was letting myself relax, erasing what I was thinking, sitting in the sunny grass of a city park near a cliff by the sea. She sat on a bench about fifteen feet away and opened a book. When I saw the title, *Moby-Dick*, I knew I'd have to start a conversation. It's one of my favorite novels, and I suspect that most people who share my enthusiasm like the book for the same reason, fascinated by the intensity of Ahab's rage at the violence of the universe, even if they're pleased when Moby-Dick finally sinks the ship. Most people read it only if it's been assigned for a class. But something about the way she was very slowly turning the pages, carefully tasting words and laughing silently from time to time, told me she was reading it by choice, as a matter of passion.

I'm not the type who can easily talk to someone I've never met before. The mere thought of a pick-up line makes me nervous, and the possibility of rejection terrifies me. But I knew she somehow knew I liked her way of turning pages, her way of shaping each word with her lips. I knew she knew I liked her lips. The ocean breeze was lovely. I told myself to take the risk.

I caught her eye when she looked in my direction. I told her a cliff by the sea was the perfect place to be reading Melville. Her eyes went back to the page. Her lips went back to shaping words. I heard the ocean crashing on the cliffs a hundred feet below. She looked up and stared at the haze where the sea became the afternoon sky. She said: Is there really a perfect place to read Melville?

I studied the mild irony on her face, thought I felt the same irony appearing on my face. I wasn't sure what it meant in either case.

She said: Wouldn't it be more accurate to say that it's impossible to read Melville? Doesn't *Moby-Dick* make reading obsolete?

I smiled: If reading is obsolete, what name should we use for what you're doing now—or rather, what you *were* doing before I so rudely interrupted?

Her tone was confrontational: Does everything need a name? Why do we assume that the presence of a name is better than its absence? And no, that's not your cue to ask me what my name is.

I played at looking hurt: You're not going to tell me?

She sounded strict: First answer the question. Does everything need a name?

I felt the strength of her mind, even though she was

only playing. I silently told myself that she was probably a graduate student in some kind of cultural studies program. I said: No. But what you're doing already has a name. Should we simply get rid of it? And if we do, what sort of epistemological gap are we creating?

She smiled: Epistemological?

I told myself that she thought I was probably a graduate student in some kind of cultural studies program. She went to the edge of the cliff and dropped her novel into the sea, walked over to me briskly, bent down and kissed me, softly at first, then with increasing strength, until she had me pinned to the ground, her tongue between my teeth. I was so shocked that at first I tried to resist, but she was clearly stronger than I was, and besides, I could feel myself getting large and hard. It wasn't just an erection. It was also an expansion, as if the seams of the moment were stretching to the bursting point, and she and I were in a small dark room in the desert, miles from human interference, and she was fucking me, alternately filling my mouth with her tongue and licking my nipples, crushing me with her arms and chest and shoulders, working my dick so fiercely that it seemed like the penis was hers. The feeling of being squashed into the carpet was painfully thrilling, something like being voluntarily raped, if such a concept can even be imagined, and obviously it can be, because it's right here, right now, wedged brazenly in that brief space which opens when something that can't exist refuses not to, an interval so electric that past and future tense disappear.

She stands and takes my hands and pulls me up and meets my eyes and says: Call me Stephanie. If you've got a name—even a fictitious name—prepare to reveal it now.

For a split second I'm not sure what to call myself, and when I tell her my name I get the feeling she doesn't believe me, leading me to wonder if the name Stephanie is fake. I'm alarmed that we seem to distrust each other so quickly, but it doesn't change the fact that we're falling in love at the speed of light. I want to be her girlfriend, she wants to be my boyfriend, a situation that's on the verge of erasing itself, but the word *erasing* quickly becomes unstable, collapsing into a story whose main character is so vividly rendered that he becomes autonomous, refusing to be the author's version of a TV sports announcer, quitting his job and rescuing a saxophone from a garbage can, practicing three hours a day for ten years, studying the works of John Coltrane, Ornette Coleman, Sonny Rollins, and Pharoah Sanders, combining their techniques to construct a solo so persuasive that it gathers rain clouds over the White House, building their electric charge until a thunderbolt forks down into the Oval Office, cleaving the president's brain, but the word *brain* quickly becomes unstable, collapsing into a story in which an intoxicated medical student who's never performed an abortion decides that he's qualified to perform one simply because he's read the appropriate pages in a textbook, and even though he follows the book precisely the patient bleeds to death, but with her final breath she tells the student that she's always been desperately in love with him, that she wanted an abortion only because the baby wasn't his, but the word *baby* quickly becomes unstable, collapsing into a story about a very shy teenage boy who goes to a party where people strip and come up with clever names for their genitals, and when he tries to leave, the toughest teenage guy in town blocks the doorway, making the shy boy shake with fear, and the girls all think his anxiety is hilarious, but on the basis of this one humiliating evening, the boy resolves to become President of the United States when he grows up, and he succeeds, but the word *become* quickly becomes unstable, collapsing into a story about a man whose dick has been frozen by a manic-depressive enchanter, so now the man spends most of his free time scrambling words and parts of words, trying to find the one combination of syllables that can break the spell, a cure he got from the enchanter himself, who insisted that he cast the spell for the sole purpose of amusing himself, the pleasure he got from going into a trance of cryptic syllables, but the word *pleasure* quickly becomes unstable, collapsing into a story about new lovers going crazy, turning their bodies into ferocious instruments of passion, comparing their sexual ecstasies to those of the Olympian gods, but Zeus and Hera get jealous, and the woman gets turned into a mad cow, the man becoming a fly that tries to avoid getting swatted away by her tail, a tale transmitting a moral warning, a sign that mortal beings need to know their limitations, need to be suspicious when their ecstasies become extreme, but the word *extreme* quickly becomes unstable, collapsing into a story about humans abducting shapeless diaphanous beings from a distant planet, performing bizarre and pointless medical experiments on their genitals, discovering in the process that Earth has long been inhabited by extraterrestrials, by a secret and sinister culture that's taken the form of human language, surviving only because humans rely on words in so many ways, but the word *surviving* quickly becomes unstable, collapsing into a story in which the characters lie nonstop, but one of them finally decides to tell a true story, a convoluted narrative in which the characters have been lying so long that they no longer know how to tell the truth, or find it so unpleasant that they'd rather just keep making things up, and the character who tells this tale has no intention of deceiving anyone, but finds herself so stuck in the habit of fabrication that the story sounds absurdly false to readers, most of whom read it several times, concluding that truth and falsehood can both be classified as performances, different ways of building an artifice whose ultimate goal is persuasion, and Stephanie talks like someone who knows that her ultimate goal is persuasion.

She backs me up against a massive palm tree, pressing her chest against my chest, her crotch against my crotch.

She says: Think of what I'm telling you as a prelude to a non-ironic love story.

I say: Are we the main characters?

She says: We create each other through the passion we create. We're not who we thought we were before the passion began.

I say: But you would agree that we're not *completely* new people?

She nods: Not *completely*.

I say: And you would agree that the feelings we exchange are *completely* authentic?

She says: They're what we truly think of each other as we share them. But much of what we say feels improvised, because the selves that speak are not selves we would have *completely* understood before the passion began. There's a girl we both become, the girl you've secretly always wanted to be, the girl you've always *been* without fully knowing it. I want to call her Megan or Pam, but you insist that her name is Loretta, and we agree on this, even though we develop different versions of what she thinks and looks like. She's part of you at first, but I imagine her so intensely that I can't get her out of my head. Soon I have no choice; she's not a visitor anymore. She's part of that blend of complexities I've learned to call my self, a new name for a girl I've been dreaming about for years.

I say: What happens next?

She says: You really want me to make that decision for both of us?

I say: Decisions terrify me. It was only with tremendous difficulty that I got myself to speak to you about Melville.

She says: So you're putting me in charge?

I say: Let's just say that I'm letting you lead me, as if we were waltzing across a nineteenth-century dance floor. I'll follow your steps, but of course the dance will be a shared experience, not something you've invented entirely on your own.

She says: Why call it a waltz? Aren't we *inventing* the dance? And if we're inventing the dance together, can we really talk about either one of us leading?

I'm falling in love with Stephanie's lips and eyes, the strength of her shoulders and arms, her carefully sculpted waist and thighs, her ass like two flexed biceps big and sharply defined from years in a gym, her way of using words as tools of power, as if she had a black belt in seduction.

I say: The way you talk, you seem to know exactly what's going on here, like you're nowhere near as surprised as I am.

She says: Let's just say I've always known I'd meet you, and everything would happen just like this. This doesn't mean we were *meant* for each other. I don't think the world is run by a cosmic chess player moving people around like knights and pawns. But you still need to answer the question: Can we really talk about either one of us leading?

I say: The notion that someone has to lead and someone has to follow is built into our culture. In fact, it's built into our language. But it may have no meaning outside our language, assuming we can truly experience anything without language.

She says: I think you're getting carried away by language.

I say: I think we're *both* getting carried away by language. That's what falling in love is all about. But if we're getting carried away, where is language taking us? And if we agree that language is better without a destination, are we both still willing to go there?

She says: How many times have you been told that you're too smart for your own good? People always told me that when I was younger.

I say: They don't anymore?

The look in her face is like a book that everyone should memorize, but the word *face* quickly becomes unstable, collapsing into a secret moment stolen from the gods, situating itself in the heat of a small dark room in the desert, drifting in the sound of venetian blinds picked up and dropped in breeze, Stephanie becoming every beautiful moment I've ever known, bulging arm and shoulder muscles rock-hard in my adoring hands, filling my mouth with a scream of pleasure so huge I can't release it, a scream that could shatter the stars or take the form of an angel to wrestle with, and Stephanie smiles at the muscle power she's built from lifting weights, the power that makes me feel so ecstatically safe when she pins my arms down. It's suddenly clear that this is the moment I've waited half a century for, a moment I've assumed would only exist in erotic dreaming. We're kissing each other so forcefully, so gracefully, that the room disappears, and everything that's not the room disappears, and only our bodies remain, suspended in the atmosphere of passion they're creating, but the word *passion* quickly becomes unstable, and its instability takes the form of a breeze on a cliff by the sea, stabilizing itself in the blue-green depth of Stephanie's eyes, redefining itself in the shine of her teeth and slightly parted lips.

She says: Tell me what you want.

I say: Isn't it obvious?

She says: Yes and no.

I say: I hate answers like that.

She says: It's not an answer.

I say: Then what is it?

She says: I'm testing you.

I say: Am I passing?

She says: Passing for what?

I say: For what you want.

She says: Tell me what I want.

I say: You want me.

She says: You want me.

I give her what can only be described as the longest kiss in the history of passion. She's got my body pinned against the tree. Her strength is overwhelming. She pulls her face away, simulating a wicked smile, and when I try to kiss her again she keeps her mouth just out of reach, using the strength in her arms to pin me firmly to the tree, very slowly licking her lips, penetrating my eyes with a commanding look, a mock invitation: *If you really think you're strong enough to kiss me, be my guest. But we both know I can keep you pinned against this tree as long as I want.* I want to sigh and melt in her arms, pleading for another kiss, knowing she'll deny it, a refusal far more delicious than any surrender could possibly be.

It's not just a sexy moment. It's a moment of self-definition. Suddenly I know myself in a way I've often imagined, but now I can *be* that self, and someone else wants me to be that self. I'm a sexy girl who wants nothing more than to faint in a powerful girl's embrace. It's more than a thought. For the first time in my life, my body feels like home. Something tells me the change is too sudden, too dramatic. Something tells me I'm being extremely neurotic, even psychotic, but the word *psychotic* quickly becomes unstable, collapsing into a story that develops like a series of doors, focusing on the girl I've become, who tells me her name is Loretta. Behind the first door there's a woman whose perfect teeth are murder weapons. She's putting a ring on Loretta's finger, promising devotion. Loretta tries to protect herself with words, but she's choked with emotion, remembering when she was fifteen, in love with her English teacher, who told her that her body looked like it might have been forty years old. Behind the second door there's a beautiful boy with delicious nipples. He makes Loretta drink a poisonous potion he's concocted. His cock is in the word *concocted*, then it's in her mouth, pronouncing itself, inseminating every cell of her body. Behind the third door, my mother unscrews the upper third of Loretta's head. Her hands are quick and skillful. There's hardly any pain at all. The windows in the background face a garden of roses and hamburger meat. The space beyond the garden is a gigantic open mouth, or a massive aquarium filled with teeth and eyeballs, or a wall of skulls. Behind the fourth door Loretta finds herself with an erection, a big surprise that quickly becomes the most beautiful thing she's ever felt, especially when she reaches down to play with herself but can't, stopped by the muscular girl she's with, who pins her hand to the mattress, challenging her to free herself and play with her dick, knowing she can't, smiling to see Loretta strain with all her strength and finally submit, and Loretta's thrilled by the size of her girlfriend's arm and shoulder muscles. Behind the fifth door, Loretta meets a man whose leg is the bone of a whale. He looks like someone harboring a violent grudge against nature, against the gods, their vast inscrutable system of limitations. He pulls Loretta close because he wants to gaze into a human eye. He says that a human eye is a magical mirror more profound than God, more beautiful than the sea or sky or memories of a distant home. She wants to tell him he needs to learn how to cry instead of just raging, but she knows that his heart is buried at the bottom of the sea. Behind the sixth door, Loretta meets herself in Stephanie's body. Stephanie remembers being four years old in her father's house, being shocked to suddenly find a blond little girl in her bedroom, someone she'd never seen before, staring out the window, turning without warning to look blankly into young Stephanie's eyes, shattering into more than a thousand pieces, quickly becoming the sound of a broom on dusty broad oak floorboards. Behind the seventh door Loretta's eyes make love to Stephanie's eyes, passion becoming tenderness bringing parts of me back from a living death, hopelessness I can't completely fathom until it's gone, leaving an empty space that the light from Stephanie's eyes begins to fill, eyes alive with tears that she's been holding back since the day she was born. My hands massaging her arms and shoulders reach up now to cup her face. I've never seen anything even half as beautiful. I can't speak. Her moistened face is everything and everywhere at once. I'm finally facing a face I can only worship and adore. I want to pluck my eyes out and never see anything else again. She takes my moistening face in her hands. The moment keeps getting larger, as if to permit a thousand words for tenderness to come into the world, as if I were nothing more than a singing head on a river of passion. But all the metaphors fail, crash like sunlit waves on jagged rocks, a hundred feet below a city park on a breezy afternoon, the feeling of Stephanie's muscular physique pressing into my body, promising to protect me from the violence of the world.

Using all my strength I finally manage to free my hands, grabbing Stephanie's wrists and trying to force them behind her back. But she quickly rips them free, grips my wrists and expands her chest, biting my mouth and firmly forcing my struggling arms back into the tree, squashing them against the rough bark, making me gasp with pain. But it's not just pain; it's also pleasure so intense it's mixed with fear, and the word *fear* quickly becomes unstable, collapsing into a story set in a park overlooking a city, naked bodies underneath a tree of midnight stars. Stephanie sits on my chest, carefully maintaining a silence that's not openly hostile, not even defensive, but clearly indicates discomfort of some kind, encased in calculated ambiguity. I'm trying to find her eyes in the dark, trying to find words to respond to what she's not quite saying. But the pressure to say the right thing makes it hard to say much of anything, so I tell her I'm scared and need to be reassured that I haven't said anything wrong. She looks up at the stars, then looks at me with troubled eyes and tells me that she loves me even though she's feeling sad. There's something unconvincing in her voice, something I want to penetrate with questions. But she gets up and walks about fifteen feet away, lighting a Lucky Strike, making it clear that she doesn't want any questions.

I stand and straighten out my pants and shirt, leaning back into the tree trunk, gazing up through branches and leaves, watching them bend in sudden breeze, making the night of stars move back and forth. Slowly the tension gripping my body relaxes, rising into what might be whispered instructions, a language I can only understand by imagining music, two jazz quartets performing the same composition at different speeds, challenging me to pay attention more carefully than I usually do, and the sound creates a gap in time, taking me away from myself by bringing me back to myself, back to where I'm warm in midday sunlight, cool in ocean breeze, loving the sound of waves on jagged rocks a hundred feet below. Stephanie sits on a bench nearby with *Moby-Dick* in her lap. Just from the way she reads, the way she forms each word with her lips, I can tell she's in love with language, that she's not just reading the book for a class. I imagine the start of a story based on a pick-up line about Melville, a story whose ultimate goal is to make the prison of gender obsolete. But when our eyes briefly meet, she doesn't look like who I thought she was. She doesn't look like anyone I can even begin to talk to. She shuts the book and walks away. I stare at her back and fake a smile. I know our eyes met perfectly at some point in the recent past, but apparently that was only one possibility. Apparently what's just happened was equally possible. But the word *apparently* quickly becomes unstable, collapsing into a tree of midnight stars and painful silence.

I finally speak to the cigarette smoke she's immersed in: I better leave in a few minutes. If I stay out any longer my fiancée might get suspicious. But I hate parting when we're not feeling fully connected.

She says: I know. But I don't know what I can say at this point to make you feel more secure. I just don't feel safe with you right now.

I say: What don't you feel safe about?

She says: Our situation.

I say: You mean—

She says: I mean, when are you going to let me leave my husband at my own pace? When are you going to stop rushing me? It's not easy, you know? I mean, he's a beautiful man who's done everything right, and I trust him more than anyone else in the world. But when I play *A Love Supreme* he gets bored. When I play it for you, it's a sacred event. You already know every note. Sure, people might laugh at me for thinking music matters so much. I couldn't care less what they think. I know what I need, and I know it's you. But will you *please* try to stop rushing me?

I want to say that I have no intention of rushing her, that I fully respect the pain of the decision she's trying to make, that I'm willing to wait as long as she needs me to wait, that in fact the waiting is good because it gives us time to learn how to care for each other. But since I've said more or less the same thing several times in the past three months, I decide I better not say it again.

Instead, I try to take her hand, but she pulls it away, so to fill the difficult silence I quickly say: I have no intention of rushing you, and I fully respect the pain of the decision you're trying to make. I'm willing to wait as long as you need me to wait. In fact, I'm not disturbed by the time we're taking. It's actually good because it gives us time to learn—

She says: You've said more or less the same thing several times in the past three months, and I know what you're really thinking. Your eyes keep telling me: *If you're really going to leave why don't you leave? How long am I supposed to believe what you say you're going to do if you're not doing it?*

I glance up at the sky and see Orion, thinking that in a work of fiction Orion might be symbolic, suggesting that we're hunting each other, hoping to catch and consume each other, savoring every bite. But I know Orion means nothing outside of a story someone else made up. I know I'd rather look up and face the night without a mythic script, meet Loretta's eyes in the drift of unconstellated starlight.

She says: Two days ago, you said you'd never leave me just because I might need time to sort through my feelings in the process of moving out. But now—

I say: I'm not saying I'm even *thinking* of leaving you. But don't ask me not to feel sad and frustrated when all I really want right now is to know I'll be with you for the rest of my life, and every day that you stay in your marriage drives me crazy because I feel like a fool waiting for something I badly want but might not ever get. Do you know how painful that is? How humiliating? It's the most difficult thing I've ever gone through.

She says: And what happens when I'm fully available? Do you get scared and run away? Are you overcome with guilt about breaking up my marriage, badly hurting my husband and your fiancée in the process?

I say: I'm more afraid that we'll wake up one day and find our passion collapsing into a story, as if it had no reality outside the words we've been using to describe it.

She says: Promise me one thing: If we ever reach a point where things are totally insane and there's nothing to do but split up, can we at least agree never to pretend that our passion hasn't been savage and lovely?

I want to say something witty about the irony of meeting the boygirl of your dreams, knowing beyond all doubt that the person is perfect, except that you're not dreaming anymore, and things are more complex when you're awake. But irony would be out of place in a world that can only exist in a non-ironic love story, so instead I say that the look in her eyes is like a fire on the ocean floor, and suddenly she's kissing me so hard I can barely stand it, using her powerful arms to force me slowly down to my knees, dropping her pants, pressing my face between her moist and muscular thighs, but the word *powerful* quickly becomes unstable, collapsing into a story about lovers climbing a mountain, planning to make love when they reach the summit, a place with a view of the ocean, mountains, and desert, but upon arriving they quickly become enraged, since the peak is already occupied by people drinking beer, talking on cell phones, blathering loudly about the Super Bowl and their favorite daytime talk shows, and the lovers try to be nice at first, smiling and making small talk, until they finally know what has to be done and pull out their guns, but the word *finally* quickly becomes unstable, collapsing into a story about an Armageddon cult, men and women preparing for the final confrontation, but when it begins with bright steam twisting down from a crack in the midnight sky, the members of the cult are suddenly horrified, awakening to the fact that they've been wrong about the crucial thing, having always thought that they were preparing to fight against evil, when the one who's leading them into battle now is the Prince of Darkness, but the word *battle* quickly becomes unstable, collapsing into a story about a teenage girl at home alone, feeling fat and sad because she doesn't have a date for the prom, watching a made-for-TV movie set on September 11, a thriller that's not really focused on a national disaster, but rather on the cleavage of the main character, a woman who works in one of the Twin Towers, anxious at her desk, refusing to answer the phone, avoiding an abusive lover she's fiercely attracted to, and she looks with rage at the sky from her window fifty-three floors up, when suddenly she sees a plane approaching, but the word *suddenly* quickly becomes unstable, collapsing into a story about a young girl asleep in an empty closet, comforting herself by curling up in the lingering smell of her father's pants and shirts and shoes, the most immediate way she can still feel close to him now that he's run off with the man of his dreams, having promised her so gently that he'd only be gone for a month or two, or at the most one year, knowing he'd be gone for good, knowing that he'd never been at home with being a father, but the word *knowing* quickly becomes unstable, collapsing into a story in which a whale destroys a whaling ship, and the only one who survives is kept afloat on an empty coffin, living to tell a tale about the captain's revenge against nature, the monomaniacal thrust of the captain's ego becoming a broken harpoon, but the word *broken* quickly becomes unstable, collapsing into my narrating voice, the sound of tires on pavement. I'm riding with the top down through a night of desert hills, warmly wrapped in a blanket wrapped in Stephanie's warm conversation, not connecting the stars with mythic or astrological narratives, not even wondering about the implications of the narrative we're designing, the limits we're constructing around our passion, since after all a narrative is a way of setting limits—excluding certain things, including others—though it should in theory be possible to make stories that erase their own boundaries, absorbing what they weren't at first including, a practice that would suggest an alternative mode of human awareness, going beyond the fact that as we construct what we experience, we focus on what seems important and filter out everything else.

Something is happening here that doesn't conform to conventional patterns, but the word *conventional* quickly becomes unstable, collapsing into a story that's not collapsing into a story, a woman performing a sacrifice, giving her anger to the gods, learning to cry instead of reacting with rage whenever she gets upset, whenever she doesn't have complete control of a situation. She watches the pattern made by the blinds and the breeze on the broad oak floorboards, a similar pattern trembling on the wall above the battered couch, as if she were listening carefully, tracking alternate versions of the same jazz composition, scored for gliding light and shade and floor and dusty silence. She lets her face grow moist with tears even though it leaves her exhausted, not sure where she is or who she is or what she might become, becoming part of a story that's erasing what it seems to be, sustaining itself with seemingly random images and events, things that don't appear to belong within its narrative limits. I don't know why they're here and not somewhere else, but if they were somewhere else I'd probably wonder why they weren't here, but the word *here* quickly becomes unstable, and again

I'm warm in the midday sunlight, cool in the ocean breeze, and Stephanie's got me pinned against the rough bark of a royal palm, fucking me with her mouth, making me feel like the sexiest girl on the planet. It's been a long time since I felt like anything more than a very incomplete man, locked away from the world by a deadly spell I somehow put on myself, even if the incantation seemed to come from an outside source, making me believe I was part of a story based on someone else, a character who made my part in the narrative seem minor, a story I was nonetheless compelled to keep telling myself, as if there were nothing outside the delusional shape it imposed on the world.

Now the voice propelling that story can't quite say what happens next. It stops, expecting everything else to stop, but things keep going, unable to resist the motion of now becoming then, or then turning into again, or here dissolving into when, a word that seems to be falling into the open jaws of a whale, or into the wine-dark space of a jazz bar after midnight, sheets of saxophone sound playing into the teeth of maniacal drumming, each instrument keeping the other from exploding into chaotic noise, jamming all night long, finally breaking out into the city, painting the dark horizon gold, charming the sun to rise like a serpent penetrating the future, decomposing into a sparsely furnished room in the desert, whispered words, a love supreme in the dark of closed venetian blinds.

We're out in the middle of nowhere because we don't want people around. We just want to fuck and sweat our way into each other's bodies forever. That's what we've been doing for more than a week, and it keeps getting better. Stephanie's on the bed with a smile that spreads the length of her body. She props her torso up with her arms and slowly licks her lips. I sweetly tuck myself beneath her chest and stroke her face. She tells me I look like the happiest girl in the world. It's a hundred degrees in the shade. I can't remember ever loving heat as much as this. Every once in a while we hear a passing car in the distance, a very non-threatening sound that only makes the silence more profound, a dot on a page that shows how perfectly blank the rest of it is. I put my arms around Stephanie's neck and rub my tits against her chest, offering my thirsting mouth, begging for a kiss. I know Loretta loves to beg for a kiss she doesn't get at first, gripping Stephanie's hard and shining arm and shoulder muscles. Then Stephanie's tongue is thrusting fiercely into Loretta's moistening mouth, making her squeal with ecstasy, making her madly beg for more, and the sound of my cute girl voice is penetrating Stephanie's helpless ear. She's guiding Loretta's penis into her moistening vagina. She's gasping. Soon she's coming and coming, coming again and again and again, erasing all separation, writing herself on the page of my body.

Neither of us ever wanted children. We'd always assumed that the stories we wrote would function as our offspring. But here on a scorching plain of sand and rocks and scrub vegetation, Stephanie can't stop smiling. Language melts in her mouth. She's thrilled to be filled with what my dick has just given her, the feeling of my life growing and glowing in her body, a new constellation carefully swimming into position, placing itself in what was once a missing part of the sky. I've never seen her so happy, so free of the skeptical limits both of us use to contain our emotions. Is it possible to feel better than this? Or would a more ecstatic state be punished by the gods? Perhaps it would, but I couldn't care less. Let the gods do all the jealous damage they want. No matter how violent they get, we've had our moment of absolute bliss. These words are proof. They grip the page, and nothing can erase them.